Butterba

Butterball

Guy de Maupassant

Translated by Andrew Brown

ET REMOTISSIMA PROPE

100 PAGES

100 PAGES
Published by Hesperus Press Limited
4 Rickett Street, London SW6 1RU
www.hesperuspress.com

These stories first published together in French as '*Boule de suif*' in 1901
This translation first published by Hesperus Press Limited, 2003

Introduction and English language translation © Andrew Brown, 2003
Foreword © Germaine Greer, 2003

Designed and typeset by Fraser Muggeridge
Printed in the United Arab Emirates by Oriental Press

ISBN: 1-84391-047-0

CONTENTS

On 17th April 1880, a letter appeared in *Le Gaulois*, ostensibly explaining the genesis of *Les Soirées de Médan*, a collection of short stories that had appeared the day before and was already causing a good deal of excitement. The letter followed an ancient literary tradition in presenting the collection as the climax of the table talk of a party of writers, including Joris-Karl Huysmans, Henri Céard, Léon Hennique and Paul Alexis, guests in Emile Zola's country house at Médan, when in fact three of the stories included in the volume had been already published. The pretext for what was in fact a collection of stories set in the context of the Franco-Prussian War was that their host proposed that they all tell a story, and set the ball rolling by telling his story of '*L'Attaque du Moulin*'. Maupassant followed with the story of the coach-load of people trying to escape the Prussian occupation after the collapse of Rouen that he had been working on for months, Huysmans with '*Sac au dos*', Céard with '*La Saignée*', Hennique with '*L'Affaire du grand 7*', and Alexis with '*Après la bataille*'. *Les Soirées de Médan* was an instant success, going through eight printings in a fortnight, and the most exciting thing in it was Maupassant's story, '*Boule de suif*' ['Butterball'] (literally 'ball of tallow').

The letter, which was actually written by Maupassant, explained that the group did not consider themselves to be a school, nor did they wish to issue a manifesto, but they were united by an instinctive reaction against the romanticism that had driven out the sharp good sense and rationality of Montaigne and Rabelais, Diderot and Voltaire. They felt, moreover, that nothing could be more extraordinary and surprising than actual events and that the duty of the artist was to understand and interpret '*l'être et la vie*', being and living, rather than to depict ideals of virtue and heroism in fantastic settings that were less interesting than actual ones.

Though Maupassant was allowed on this occasion to speak for the naturalist school, he was much less a follower of Zola than he was of his old family friend and mentor Gustave Flaubert, who corrected the proofs of '*Boule de suif*' for him. Indeed, Maupassant took the occasion of the letter to *Le Gaulois* to ridicule Zola, describing him as eating 'enough for three ordinary novelists' and blazing away with his gun at clumps of grass because his disciples told him they were birds. Zola's huge epics, that were meant to display the workings of an entire society, have little in common with Maupassant's cool, understated and economic cameos of everyday monstrousness. Zola's characters convince because they are representative, Maupassant's because they are as varied and peculiar, and as dispassionately viewed, as the organisms in a drop of pond water.

As a young soldier, Maupassant had been involved in the rout of the French at Rouen in December 1870 and had witnessed the behaviour of well-to-do citizens attempting to save their own skins. Butterball has been identified as Adrienne Annonciade Legay, mistress of a businessman who had been drafted at Le Havre; she travelled through occupied Normandy in 1871 trying to find him, apparently without success, because she died destitute in 1892, twelve years after Maupassant had made his literary reputation by telling her story. Carré-Lamadon is a certain Pouyer-Quertier, president of the chamber of commerce of Rouen and mayor of Fleury-sur-Andelle; Cornudet is Cordhomme, second husband of Maupassant's aunt.

These factoids tell us what we already know, that there is

nothing intrinsically improbable in Maupassant's story or his characters. His descriptions of the shabby equipage and its grotesque inhabitants have the exaggerated clarity of drawings by Goya, or perhaps, Daumier. From the first, Butterball is presented as an object for consumption, as appetising as a window display in a provincial charcuterie, and throughout the crazy journey it is her fatness that feeds the parasites that surround her who, having consumed all the delicious foodstuffs she provides, feed her to the German soldier, and then ignore her as beneath their contempt. Though the story is told with genial good humour and apparent gusto, it is as damning an indictment of provincial society as anything Flaubert might have written. The coach, dragged so slowly through the snow by its dispirited horses, is Maupassant's version of the ship of fools.

By 1880, Maupassant was already showing signs of the syphilitic neuropathy that would result in his insanity and death in 1893, less than four years after that of his younger brother, Hervé, who was similarly afflicted. It would seem that both sons of Laure le Poittevin, who separated from her husband when Guy was ten, apparently as a consequence of his womanising, were infected with syphilis at birth. As syphilis was wrongly considered hereditable, it would not be surprising if Maupassant believed that there was nothing to be done for him once symptoms had appeared, and that through no fault of his own, he was doomed to the madness and physical torment that was so soon to overtake him. He sought no treatment for the cardiac pains and skin lesions that he suffered in 1876, but simply ate, drank, swived and worked more intemperately than ever, though he had yet to have any work published. '*Boule de suif*' changed all that; partly because of Flaubert's enthusiasm for this small masterpiece,

Maupassant was in great demand. Flaubert's death from a massive stroke less than a month after his protégé's debut devastated Maupassant and his syphilitic symptoms returned with a vengeance. Very much aware that he was living on borrowed time, he quit his job at the Ministry of Public Instruction and devoted himself to hard work and high living.

By December 1883, when '*Première neige*' ['First Snow'] appeared in *Le Gaulois*, Maupassant was making a comfortable living by his pen; besides his regular appearances in *Le Gaulois*, he was also contributing stories to *Gil Blas* under the name of Maufrigneuse. The proceeds allowed him to keep a manservant and buy a yacht which he kept on the Côte d'Azur. In 1885 he published the first collections of his stories, *Contes du jour et de la nuit* in which '*Rose*' was reprinted, and *Toine*, in which '*La Dot*' ['The Dowry'], '*Le Lit 29*' ['Bed 29'] and '*L'Aveu*' ['The Confession'] were reprinted. ('*Première neige*' was never reprinted in his lifetime.)

In his letter to *Le Gaulois*, Maupassant claimed that he did not understand the words 'realism' and 'idealism'. Because he is not an idealist he is generally taken to be a realist, but his vignettes of events, whether in Normandy or on the Côte d'Azur or the streets of Paris, are by no means snapshots or slices of life. What Maupassant constructs by carefully weaving strands of the visible with the presumed and the predigested are icons of ambiguity, in which there can be neither right nor innocence. All his characters are deluded, all are manipulative and all are overtaken by events. There is no triumph and no tragedy. Céleste Malivoire's pregnancy is a matter of no moment, embedded as it is in the blaze of the summer countryside. The woman in 'First Snow' is less the victim of her husband's insensitivity and meanness than of her own indolence and self-will; the upshot, death, will be the same in any case. The outcome of 'Bed 29' is as unknowable and unthinkable as Maupassant's own fate as a syphilitic. The curious magic of Maupassant is that his basically savage view of life is expressed with such zest and finesse that we cannot doubt that, however blighted by our own ignorance and self-deceiving, or by misfortune, anguish and disease, life is fascinating, absorbing and utterly worth living.

– Germaine Greer, 2003

Fat is a feminist issue. Why else does Maupassant make the prostitute in one of his most famous stories, 'Butterball', excessively well endowed with feminine tissue? This is a story about food, sex, and politics, and about the impossibility of separating them out or establishing a secure order of priority between them. Which comes first, need (the need to eat, the need to stave off or compromise with an occupying military force if one is to survive), or desire (the desire for other bodies, the more symbolic desire for recognition of oneself as a full person)? It is a story about mouths: they can kiss, they can eat, and they can talk – above all, in this story, they can utter pretentious political jargon, hypocritical pieties, coarse and cynical jokes, and wheedling persuasions. Mouths are the most obvious place in the body where we take in (food) and give out (words), or both at once (kisses): we can grant our mouths and their concomitant gifts to others, or we can withhold them. The mouth is where we decide whether or not we are going to be fat, but also whether or not to be generous – to ourselves (when we stuff our faces) or to others (when we utter the words 'have some yourself!'). Fat causes anxiety because it can signify health (a fat person is not apparently starving to death) and its opposite (obesity).

Butterball's name makes her sound appetising, though more in the English (or American) equivalent I have chosen than the original French. Maupassant calls her *Boule de suif*; like 'butterball' this can mean, colloquially, a fat person, but *'boule'* means anything round, and *'suif'* means tallow or candle grease. So she is as much a ball of tallow as of butter. When at the end of the story she dissolves into tears of rage and betrayal, she is melting like a ball of butter in a chicken, or shedding wax like a burning candle. (There are other connotations in her name. '*Recevoir un suif*' is to get a dressing down, a telling-off; '*chercher du suif*' is to be spoiling for a fight; and '*suiffard*' means toff, or swell, as well as a cheat (at cards) or a quarrelsome person. *Boule de suif* certainly shows her 'irascible' independence of spirit, and she finds herself in the midst of toffs (while being capable of a certain aristocratic disdain herself); the others in the party play cards, and two of them (the Loiseau couple) cheat. So *Boule de suif* is one of those names that tells more of the story than might first appear.)

Butterball's name focuses on her most obvious physical attribute. It is noteworthy that many of the names used to refer to fat people ('dumpling', 'tub of lard') make of them perspicuous examples of Feuerbach's materialist maxim: 'You are what you eat' (in German: '*Man ist, was man isst*'). They are as fat as if they had eaten great balls of butter (or huge tubs of lard); they look like what they have eaten; and maybe they in turn would be good to eat. Very early on in the story, Loiseau (the wag in the tale) suggests that the starving passengers leaving Prussian-occupied Rouen for the coast might eat the fattest person there – Butterball, of course. The hint of cannibalism is obvious, and eat her they do: or rather, she feeds them, not with her own body but with the food that her body has earned in its trade as a prostitute. When there is only one cup for the travellers to drink the wine she offers round, fastidiously wiping the rim as they do so, there is the hint of a eucharistic topos: this is my body. It is certainly her body that saves them again later on, when she is finally persuaded to yield to the Prussian's lusts so that he will release them all from hostage. She gives, as it were, her body to be consumed by the enemy on behalf of her fellow-travellers – who then, of course, refuse to share their food with her once they are back in the coach and free to resume their journey. She is made ambiguous in the way all fat people arouse contradictory moral responses; they are simultaneously generous and selfish, they celebrate the circulation of food and property (Rabelaisian feasts, Falstaffian anarchy) and hoard it in their own flesh; they are not bothered about body boundaries, being all too happy to let it all hang out of the stays and corsets that truss up the bourgeoisie in its strait-laced morality. A fat woman like Butterball rouses particularly fraught feelings in the situation of the story: her plumpness is maternal (pregnant women are fat, she has a nice round bosom – even though she seems to have farmed out her own child for others to bring up) but also insulting (she – the hussy! – has obviously, given her girth, not gone short of food, and to crown it all has remembered to bring provisions on her journey while we, upstanding citizens with other anxieties and our minds on higher things, forgot). It is as if her initial generosity to the other travellers were not really much of a sacrifice: like all good mothers, she appears to produce food quite spontaneously, out of the substance of her own body, without having to work for it. But she *has* worked for it, of course. She is a woman who is usually generous with her favours – that is what her companions think when they are feeling hostile towards her: all that flesh, plenty to go round, why be mean to the Prussian when she's thrown herself at every other man in Rouen? So in their eyes she turns, capriciously, into a bad mother, refusing the sexual nourishment of her body to the man who has power over all of them.

So Maupassant's story touches, lightly but suggestively, on the overlap between fat and sexuality (it is interesting that, unlike in our own slimline age, Butterball's fatness is never seen as making her undesirable – quite the contrary). There is, admittedly, nothing particularly new in the theme. More subtle is his depiction of the shifting alliances between the characters who are forced to share the coach and then the dingy hotel in their flight from occupied Rouen. All the respectable men line up against the hairy lefty, Cornudet, all Pale Ale and Revolution; their wives form a phalanx of matrimonial righteousness against Butterball. But the possibility of common ground being established between the prostitute and the democrat is undermined when she turns out to be a Bonapartist, fiercely committed to Louis Napoleon who has just fallen from power, and thus on the opposite side of the political spectrum from Cornudet. Her imperial allegiances bring her into the camp of the conservative women: politics has momentarily cut across the boundaries of class and respectability. Still, Cornudet, unfazed by bourgeois proprieties, tries to get off with her, both in the coach and again, more explicitly, in the hotel. He is rebuffed, Butterball indignantly pointing out that it is not the time or the place for fornication: there might even be a Prussian in the next room! When later on she is forced to yield to the Prussian's demands, Cornudet alone berates his fellow-travellers who are tipsily celebrating their imminent liberation and indulging in lascivious banter as Butterball's sacrifice is consummated in the room overhead. But Loiseau spitefully attributes this moral indignation to Cornudet's own foiled lusts, and even to jealousy – which may or may not be true. It nonetheless deprives the story of anyone (apart from Butterball) able to occupy the high moral ground, and if she is allowed to occupy that eminence, it is only as a victim; the good, as ever, are the powerless. The other travellers draw together in contempt for her at the end of the story, when having served her purpose as self-sacrificing saviour she can be reconsigned to the category of common tart. Meanwhile, Cornudet (whose sympathies for her do not extend to the offer of one of his boiled eggs now that she is starving) riles the bourgeoisie by inanely humming the Marseillaise (still, in 1870–1, subversively revolutionary in its connotations) for the rest of their journey. But this is not much use to Butterball, and the final vignette (the useless democrat, the 'respectable' characters full of frozen disdain and anxieties about the post-imperial order, and the prostitute who has gone against her principles to sleep with the enemy, forced as she is to be a collaborator so as to be patriotic) is a triangle of alienation.

'Confession' and 'First Snow' are slighter pieces, though they too counterpoint human beings with their environment: the Normandy landscape is lush in the first and frozen in the second, but in either case the inhabitants are tight-fisted – in the first story amiably and comically, in the second (where the husband refuses to furnish his draughty château with a stove to protect his ailing wife from the cold) to the point of criminal neglect. In 'First Snow' the woman is isolated, as she is in most of these stories: by her profession as prostitute, or by being locked into a marriage where she has no real voice – in 'The Dowry', by being married off to someone who betrays her almost immediately. (Walter Benjamin contemplated writing a study of Maupassant that would have focused on the theme of the hunter as a type now as prevalent in the city as in the country: in 'The Dowry' we have a bounty-hunter of a particularly successful kind, and he bags his catch in the very heart of Paris.) As so often, Maupassant shows the sheer ugliness of bourgeois marriage.

'Rose' crams into its narrow compass a bewildering range of themes. The festival of flowers in Cannes, where the lower orders are cordoned off from the bourgeoisie who parade up and down playfully exchanging botanical missiles, is used as the frame for an anecdote as complex as anything in Jean Genet, adept as he was at exploring the link between flowers, masquerade, and desire. For 'Rose', the character on whom the story turns, turns out to be a 'phenomenon', a rose with a thorn, a rose that by another name smells far less sweet (but does create an erotic frisson of ambiguity). Again boundaries and their transgression are explored, rapidly and allusively: there is a blending of the law-abiding and the criminal, male and female, upper- and lower-class, heterosexual and homosexual (what kind of desire is at work when Rose massages 'her' mistress?).

Finally, in 'Bed 29', Maupassant returns to the Franco-Prussian War and shows how another 'woman of easy virtue' reacts to the invasion, in a particularly effective form of collaboration-and-resistance. Here, as elsewhere, Maupassant is as economical with words as his fellow-Normans were with more concrete possessions, but the grim depiction of the syphilitic ward, and the laconic evocation of the cowardice ultimately shown by the colonel (an initially rather attractive comic figure), are powerful, especially if one bears in mind what a delayed-action time bomb Irma's contribution to the war effort really is, and wonders just how many Prussian officers, having triumphantly returned back home to Berlin or Rostock or Magdeburg, will start to feel really not very well round about 1880. (As the Colonel's hair-loss may itself be a symptom of syphilis, the origin of Irma's infection is in any case less easy to pinpoint than she suggests.)

There is a biographical poignancy to this story: Maupassant, in his younger days just as athletic and vigorous as the colonel, himself succumbed to syphilis, of a kind even more ghastly than Irma's in that it affected his mental health too.

This dedicated oarsman, womaniser, and restless traveller died at the age of forty-two, insane; he was a commercial writer of enormous popular success, but in some ways yet another of nineteenth-century France's *poètes maudits*. A poet? It is true that the human failings of these stories are generally humdrum, and the one real example of heroism (that of Irma) must have provoked a shudder of awed disgust among its first readers. Henry James, not prone to excessive puritanism, voiced a common contemporary reaction to Maupassant when he proclaimed him, in his best English-gentlemanly manner, 'a cad – of genius'. A bounder of talent, more like. But a poet, too, at times. For there is a tenuous poetry in the interplay between the bare annotation of all-too-human foibles on the one hand (so unadorned and geometrical in the case of 'Butterball', with its unnerving symmetry, as to resemble a parable, or one of the clear-eyed and disabused fables of La Fontaine) and the natural world on the other. Nietzsche (another syphilitic *poète maudit*) thought much more highly of Maupassant than did James, and put his finger (albeit for his own ideological reasons) on Maupassant's 'Latin' or Mediterranean aspect – the sunshine, the vitality, the love of clear forms as found in warm southern climes. But emotional warmth, in Maupassant, is in short supply: the Normandy countryside is as fertile as the peasant girl in 'A Confession', but her very fecundity is the product of stingy penny-pinching calculation; the Riviera is a paradise for the protagonist of 'First Snow', but she has come there to die, escaping too late from the icy chill in her husband's château (and heart). Even the flower festival in Cannes ('Rose') seems a nastily elitist affair for the idle upper classes, just as Rose herself, as a diligent and attentive servant pampering a lazy and sensual mistress, is – for all the pleasant sexual ambivalence in the story – as conformist as she is (given what we eventually learn about her) subversive. In 'Butterball', above all, there is a poetry in the way the snow of the outer world duplicates the ice in the hearts of the characters, cold and calculating as they are. Butterball's tears alone are not enough to melt them. Auden, in his elegy on Yeats, gave a Blakean note to the chill that lies on human relations (as was all too obviously the case at the time of writing of the poem, February 1939), where he speaks of the 'seas of pity' being 'locked and frozen'. The young Franz Kafka asked, in a letter to his friend Oskar Pollack, what was the point of reading books unless they bite and sting us. 'A book must be the axe for the frozen sea in us.' It is not only Normans who are stingy, or members of the French nineteenth century who were so blind to their inner contradictions and hypocrisy. It is not just the frozenness of the winter landscape in 'Butterball', nor even the frozenness of human relations in the alienated society that Maupassant depicted, and in which we still live, that needs to be thawed (or broken up with an axe), but the frozen sea in us – hypocrite readers as we are.

– Andrew Brown, 2003

Note on the Text:
The text I have used is: Guy de Maupassant, *Boule de Suif*, edited by Louis Forestier (Paris: Gallimard, 1999).

Butterball

Butterball

For several days in succession, tattered remnants of the defeated army had been passing through the town. They were no longer troops, but rampaging hordes. The men had long, filthy beards, their uniforms were in shreds, and they advanced slackly, without a flag, without a regiment. All of them seemed crushed, broken, incapable of thought or resolve, marching merely out of habit, and dropping with fatigue the minute they stopped. The greater number were reservists, pacific characters and quiet well-to-do men, bent beneath the weight of their rifles; or alert little militiamen, quick to panic and easily roused to enthusiasm, as ready for attack as for flight; then, in their midst, a few red-trousered soldiers, the debris of a division that had been given a good thrashing in some great battle; sombre artillerymen marching in line with these various foot-soldiers; and, at times, the shining helmet of a dragoon, dragging his feet along and barely keeping up with the lighter step of the infantry.

Legions of irregular combatants bearing heroic names: the 'Avengers of Defeat' – the 'Citizens of the Tomb' – the 'Companions of Death' – went by in turn, looking like bandits.

Their leaders, formerly cloth- or seed-merchants, or dealers in tallow or soap, were occasional warriors, who had been appointed officers because of their wealth or the length of their moustaches. Loaded with weapons, flannel and gold braid, they spoke with booming voices, discussed plans of campaign, and declared that they could, all by themselves, support France in its death-agony on their boastful shoulders; but they were sometimes frightened of their own soldiers, men fit only for the gallows, often excessively brave, always indulging in pillage and debauchery.

The Prussians were about to enter Rouen, people said.

The National Guard, which had, for the last two months, been carrying out very cautious reconnoitring in the nearby woods, sometimes shooting their own sentries, and ready to leap into action every time a little rabbit stirred in the undergrowth, had returned to hearth and home. Their weapons, their uniforms, all the murderous paraphernalia with which they had been striking fear along all the milestones of the highways for three leagues around had suddenly disappeared.

The last French soldiers had finally crossed the Seine to reach Pont-Audemer via Saint-Sever and Bourg-Achard; and, walking behind them, the general, in despair, unable to try anything with this ragged assortment, himself swallowed up in the overwhelming rout of a people used to victory and now disastrously beaten despite its legendary bravery, made his way along on foot between two aides-de-camp.

Then a profound calm, a terrified and silent sense of foreboding had come to hover above the city. Many pot-bellied men from the middle class, emasculated by commerce, awaited the victors anxiously, trembling at the idea that their roasting-spits or their big kitchen knives might be viewed as weapons.

Life seemed to have come to a standstill; the shops were closed, the streets mute. Sometimes an inhabitant, intimidated by this silence, would quickly slip along the walls.

The anguish of expectation made them desire the enemy's arrival.

On the afternoon of the day following the departure of the French troops, a few uhlans, emerging from God knows

4

where, swept through the city. Then, a little later, a dark mass came down from the slopes of the Sainte-Catherine district, while two other streams of invaders appeared coming along the Darnétal and Bois-Guillaume roads. The vanguards of the three bodies, at exactly the same moment, joined forces on the square in front of the town hall; and, along all the neighbouring roads, the German army started to arrive, battalion after battalion, making the cobbles echo to their harsh, rhythmic steps.

Commands, shouted out in an unknown guttural tongue, rose along the houses which seemed dead and deserted, while from behind the closed shutters, eyes peeped out at these victorious men, masters of the city, of the fortunes and lives in it, by 'right of conquest'. The inhabitants in their darkened rooms were struck by the panic induced by natural cataclysms, by those great murderous upheavals of the earth, against which all wisdom and all strength are useless. For the same sensation reappears each time that the established order of things is overturned, when security no longer exists and all that was protected by the laws of men or those of nature finds itself at the mercy of a fierce and mindless brutality. The earthquake that crushes an entire populace beneath their collapsing houses; the overflowing river which rolls along in its torrent drowned peasants with the carcasses of cattle and the beams torn from rooftops; or the glorious army massacring those who put up any resistance, leading the others away as prisoners, pillaging in the name of the sabre and giving thanks to a God with the sound of the cannon – all are so many terrible scourges which confound any belief in eternal justice, any trust that we have learnt to place in Heaven's protection and man's reason.

But at every door, small detachments were starting to

5

knock, before disappearing into the houses. After invasion came occupation. The vanquished now had to fulfil their duty of showing themselves gracious towards the victors.

After a while, once the first terror had evaporated, a new calm set in. In many households, the Prussian officer ate at table with the family. He was sometimes well brought-up, and out of politeness would express his sympathy for France and his repugnance at having to take part in this war. People felt grateful to him for these sentiments; then, after all, maybe they might need his protection one day or another. By dealing tactfully with him, they might get away with a few men less to feed. And why hurt the feelings of someone on whom they were entirely dependent? To behave like that would be an act less of bravery than of rashness – and rashness is no longer a failing of the Rouen middle classes, as it had been at the time of the heroic defences in which their city once distinguished itself. Furthermore, drawing on the supreme reason of French urbanity, people told themselves that, after all, it was perfectly permissible to be polite at home so long as they did not show themselves familiar with the foreign soldier in public. Once outside the house, they no longer wanted to know him, but indoors they were quite prepared to have a chat, and the German would stay on a little longer each evening, warming himself at the communal hearth.

The city itself started, little by little, to regain its ordinary appearance. The French still emerged only rarely, but the streets were crawling with Prussian soldiers. In any case, the officers of the Blue Hussars, arrogantly scraping their great tools of death along the cobbles, did not seem to have for the ordinary citizens much more contempt than had the light infantrymen who, the year before, had been drinking in the same cafés.

Nonetheless, there was something in the air, something subtle and unfamiliar, a strange and intolerable atmosphere, like a spreading odour, the odour of invasion. It filled the houses and the public places, changed the way food tasted, gave people the impression they were travelling far from home among dangerous barbarian tribes.

The victors were demanding money, a lot of money. The inhabitants always paid; in any case, they were rich. But the more a Norman merchant is rolling in money, the more he suffers from having to make any sacrifice, or see any scrap of his fortune passing into the hands of someone else.

However, two or three leagues downriver from the city, towards Croisset, Dieppedalle or Biessart, the bargemen and fishers would often dredge up from the depths the corpse of some German, all swollen in his uniform, killed with a thrust of the knife or a well-aimed kick, his head crushed by a stone – or sometimes he had been pushed into the water from a bridge. The muddy river buried these obscure acts of vengeance, savage and legitimate, anonymous deeds of heroism, silent assaults, more perilous than battles fought out in the open, and without any of their resounding glory.

For hatred towards the Foreigner always causes a few intrepid characters to take up arms, ready as they are to die for an idea.

Finally, as the invaders, although admittedly imposing their inflexible discipline on the city, perpetrated none of the horrors that rumour had ascribed to them all along their triumphal march, people grew emboldened, and the need to do business again started to weigh on the hearts of the local merchants. Some of them had major business interests in Le Havre, which was still occupied by the French army, and they wanted to try and reach this port by travelling overland to Dieppe, where they would take a boat.

They used the influence of the German officers they had got to know, and authorisation for them to leave the city was obtained from the general-in-chief.

So it was that a big four-horse coach was reserved for the trip, and ten persons registered with the coachman; and they resolved to leave one Tuesday morning, before daybreak, so as to avoid attracting a crowd of onlookers.

A frost had frozen the earth solid for days now, and on Monday, around three o'clock, big black clouds coming from the north brought snow, which fell uninterruptedly all evening and all night.

At half-past four in the morning, the travellers gathered in the yard of the Hôtel de Normandie, where they were to board the stagecoach.

They were still very sleepy, and shivered with cold under their wraps. They could barely see each other in the darkness; and the heavy winter clothes they had put on made them all look like overweight priests with their long cassocks. But two men recognised one another, a third came up to them, and they started chatting.

'I'm taking my wife along,' said one.

'So am I.'

'Me too.'

The first added, 'We're not coming back to Rouen, and if the Prussians move towards Le Havre, we'll go to England.'

They all had the same plans, being of similar mind.

But the coach was still not being harnessed. A little lamp, carried by a stable-boy, emerged from time to time from one dark doorway, only to disappear immediately into another. Horses' hooves stamped on the ground, the noise muffled by the stable-litter, and a man's voice talking to the animals and swearing could be heard from the depths of the building. A low jangle of bells announced the fact that the harnesses were being positioned; this jangle soon became a clear and continuous ringing, following the rhythm of the horses' movements, sometimes stopping, then starting up again with a sudden shake accompanied by the dull thud of an iron-shod clog clomping across the ground.

The door suddenly closed. All noise ceased. The frozen citizens had fallen silent; they stood there, motionless and stiff.

An uninterrupted curtain of white snowflakes glimmered ceaselessly as it fell to the earth; it effaced shapes and covered everything with a foamy, icy powder; and in the great silence of the city, calm and buried under the winter weather, all that could be heard was this indescribable, vague, floating whisper, the noise of falling snow, more of a sensation than a noise, the intermingling of light atoms that seemed to be filling the whole of space and blanketing the world.

The man reappeared with his lamp, pulling along at the end of a rope an unwilling and refractory horse. He set him to the shafts, attached the traces, and spent a long time going round making sure that the harness was secure, for he had only one hand free, as the other was carrying his lamp. As he was going to fetch the second horse, he noticed all these motionless travellers, already white with snow, and said to them, 'Why don't you get into the coach? At least you'll be sheltered there.'

They had not thought of this, no doubt, and they leapt at the chance. The three men installed their wives in the back of the coach, and got up after them; then the other shapeless and hidden figures in turn took the last seats without exchanging a word.

The floor was covered with straw and their feet snuggled into it. The ladies at the back, who had brought along little copper footwarmers heated by chemical fuel, lit these apparatuses and spent some time enumerating their advantages in low voices, repeating to each other things that they had already known for a long time.

Finally, once the coach had been harnessed with six horses instead of four because it was harder to pull, a voice outside asked, 'Has everyone got in?' A voice inside replied, 'Yes.' And off they went.

The coach rolled on ever so slowly, at the most laboured pace. The wheels sank into the snow; the whole vehicle emitted groans and muffled creaks; the horses slipped, panted, steamed; and the coachman's giant whip continually cracked, flew out on this side and that, curling and uncurling like a slender snake, and suddenly lashing a firm round crupper that then tautened in a more violent effort.

But the day was imperceptibly dawning. Those light snowflakes that one traveller, a pure-blooded Rouennais, had compared to a shower of cotton, were no longer falling. A murky light was filtering through heavy dark clouds that brought out even more the dazzling whiteness of the countryside where there sometimes appeared a line of tall trees decked with hoar frost, and sometimes a hovel wearing a hood of snow.

In the coach, they looked at each other curiously, in the wan light of dawn.

Right at the back, in the best seats, M. and Mme Loiseau, wholesale wine merchants from the rue Grand-Pont, were sitting opposite each other dozing.

The former clerk of a boss who had been ruined in business, Loiseau had bought up his stock and made his fortune. He sold very poor wine very cheaply to the small countryside retailers and enjoyed the reputation among his friends and acquaintances of being a sly old fox, a real Norman, full of cunning and joviality.

His reputation as a swindler was so well established that one evening, in the *préfecture*, M. Tournel, the author of fables and songs, a man of biting and subtle wit, a local celebrity, had proposed to the ladies who he could see were starting to drowse, that they play a game of '*Loiseau vole*': the witticism itself *flew* through the prefect's drawing-rooms; then, having reached those in the rest of the town, made everyone in the province laugh for a whole month until their jaws ached.[1]

Loiseau was, besides that, famous for his practical jokes of every kind, the tricks he played both pleasant and unpleasant; and nobody could mention him without immediately adding, 'He's priceless, is old Loiseau.'

Diminutive in stature, he presented a prominent paunch, topped with a red face, framed by two sets of greying side-whiskers.

His wife, tall, sturdy, resolute, with a loud voice and a mind soon made up, brought order and good bookkeeping to the firm, while he enlivened it with his merry activities.

Next to them, more dignified, belonging to a higher caste, sat M. Carré-Lamadon, a considerable personage, well established in the cotton business, proprietor of three spinning-mills, officer of the Legion of Honour and member of the General Council. He had remained, throughout the Empire period, at the head of the most loyal opposition solely in order to ensure that he would be paid more to give his support to the same cause that he combated 'with courteous weapons', as he himself put it. Mme Carré-Lamadon, much younger than her husband, continued to be a comforting presence to officers from good families stationed in Rouen.

She was sitting opposite her husband, all small and dainty, a pretty little thing, bundled up in her furs, and gazing with a woebegone expression at the dismal interior of the coach.

The people next to her, the Count and Countess Hubert de Bréville, bore one of the oldest and noblest names in Normandy. The Count, an old gentleman of distinguished demeanour, attempted to bring out, by affecting similar dress, his natural resemblance to good King Henri IV who, following a legend that redounded to the family's glory, had made a lady of Bréville pregnant: her husband, by virtue of this deed, had become a count and the governor of a province.

Having M. Carré-Lamadon as a colleague on the General Council, Count Hubert represented the Orleanist party in the *département*. The story of his marriage to the daughter of a small shipowner from Nantes had always been shrouded in mystery. But as the Countess bore herself like a lady, received her guests better than anyone else, and was even said to have been the lover of one of the sons of Louis-Philippe, the whole nobility fêted her, and her salon remained the premier salon in the region, the only one in which old habits of gallantry were preserved, and to which it was difficult to gain access.

The fortune of the de Bréville couple, all in real estate, amounted, it was said, to five hundred thousand pounds in revenue.

These six persons formed the solid ballast of the coach, the section that represented well-to-do society of independent means, serene and strong: decent people, pillars of the establishment, imbued with Religion and High Principles.

By a strange quirk of fate all the women found themselves sitting on the same side, and the Countess had two other women next to her: two nuns who were telling their beads over and over, mumbling 'Our Fathers' and 'Hail Marys'. One was old, with a face pitted by smallpox, as if she had received a point-blank barrage of grapeshot full in the face. The other, very frail, had a pretty, sickly face and the chest of a consumptive, ravaged by that all-devouring faith which makes martyrs and mystics.

Opposite the two nuns, a man and a woman drew everyone's eyes to them.

The man, a well-known character, was Cornudet the 'democrat', the terror of respectable folk. For twenty years, he had been dipping his great red beard in the beer glasses of all the democratic cafés. He had, with his brothers and friends, swallowed up quite a large fortune inherited from his father, a former confectioner, and he had impatiently waited for the Republic to arrive, so he could at last gain the place merited by so many revolutionary acts of consumption. On 4th September, as a consequence of some practical joke perhaps, he had been led to believe that he had been appointed prefect, but when he tried to assume his functions, the lads in the office, who had remained in sole charge of the building, refused to recognise him, and he was forced to beat a retreat.[2] Anyhow he was a good sort, inoffensive and ready to give his services, and he had busied himself with incomparable ardour in organising the defence. He had ensured that holes were dug in the plains, all the young trees in the nearby forests were cut down, ambushes were set on all the roads, and at the approach of the enemy, satisfied with his preparations, he had fallen back with all due haste onto the city. Now he thought he could make himself more useful in Le Havre, where new retrenchments were going to be necessary.

The woman, one of the so-called 'women of easy virtue', was famous for her precocious corpulence, which had earned her the nickname of Butterball. She was small, round all over, as fat as lard, with puffed-up fingers congested at the joints so they looked like strings of short sausages; with a glossy, taut skin, and a huge and prominent bosom straining out from beneath her dress, she nonetheless remained an appetising and much sought-after prospect, so fresh that she was a pleasure to see. Her face was a russet apple, a peony bud about to flower; above, two magnificent black eyes opened wide, shaded by great thick eyelashes that cast a shadow all around; and below, a charming mouth, with pursed lips all moist for kissing, well furnished with gleaming microscopic baby teeth.

Furthermore she was said to be full of the most inestimable talents.

As soon as she was recognised, a low murmur ran from one respectable woman to the next, and the words 'prostitute' and 'a public scandal' were whispered so loud that she looked up. Then she let her eyes travel across her fellow-travellers with such a bold and provocative gaze that a great silence immediately fell, and all present lowered their eyes, with the exception of Loiseau, who ogled her with a leer.

But conversation soon resumed between the three ladies whom the presence of this hussy had suddenly made friendly, almost intimate with each other. It seemed to them that it was their duty to barricade themselves behind their wifely dignity in the face of this shameless whore; for law-abiding love always looks down its nose at its free-and-easy colleague.

The three men too, drawn together by the shared sense of being on the conservative side opposite Cornudet, talked money, referring to the poor with a certain tone of disdain. Count Hubert described the damage that the Prussians had inflicted on him, the losses that would result from the stolen livestock and the lost harvests, with the self-assurance of a grand seigneur, a millionaire ten times over, who would be adversely affected by these ravages for perhaps a year, if that. M. Carré-Lamadon, facing many trials and tribulations in the cotton industry, had taken the precaution of sending six hundred thousand francs to England, a little something put by for a rainy day. As for Loiseau, he had taken pains to sell to the French Commissariat all the ordinary wine he still had in his cellars, so that the State owed him a huge sum that he was expecting to get his hands on once he reached Le Havre.

And all three of them darted friendly glances at each other. Although coming from different milieux, they felt that they were part of the brotherhood of money, the great freemasonry of the haves, who, every time they put their hands in their trouser pockets, let you hear the clink of gold coins.

The coach was making such slow progress that at ten in the morning they had travelled less than four leagues. The men got out three times to climb the hillsides on foot. They were starting to become anxious, for they were supposed to be having lunch at Tostes and now they were starting to think they would not get there before nightfall. They were all looking out for a wayside inn, when the coach foundered in a deep snowdrift and they took two hours to dig it out.

Their appetite was growing, making them feel light-headed; and not a single cheap restaurant or tavern was visible, for the approach of the Prussians and the passage of the starving French troops had scared off all commerce.

The men went to try and find provisions in the wayside farms, but they could not even find any bread, for the mistrustful peasants concealed their reserves for fear of being pillaged by the soldiers who, without a bite to eat, would forcibly make off with anything they discovered.

Around one o'clock in the afternoon, Loiseau announced that he really was starting to feel a damned great hole in his stomach. Everyone else, too, had been suffering for a long time, and as the violent need to eat continued to increase, it ended up killing off all conversation.

From time to time someone would yawn; someone else almost immediately did likewise; and each of them in turn, depending on their character, their knowledge of the proprieties, and their social position, would open their mouths noisily or modestly, hurriedly holding their hands in front of the gaping holes from which clouds of steam emerged.

Butterball, on several occasions, leant down as if she were looking for something beneath her skirts. She hesitated for a second, looked round at her neighbours, then tranquilly sat up again. They all had pale, drawn faces. Loiseau asserted that he would pay a thousand francs for a knuckle of ham. His wife made a gesture as if to protest, then she calmed down. She always suffered when she heard people discussing money being wasted, and she could not even understand why anyone might joke about such a subject. 'The fact is, I'm not feeling very well,' said the Count. 'Why didn't I think to bring some food?' Everyone else likewise reproached themselves.

However, Cornudet had a flask full of rum; he offered it round; it was coldly refused. Loiseau alone took a couple of sips, and when he returned the flask, he thanked him: 'It's nice, you know; it warms you up and it takes your mind off your appetite.' The alcohol put him in a good mood and he suggested that they do as on the little ship in the song, and eat the plumpest of the travellers. This indirect allusion to Butterball shocked the better brought-up people. They made no reply; Cornudet alone smiled. The two nuns had stopped mumbling their rosary, and sat upright and motionless, their hands folded deep into their great sleeves, obstinately lowering their eyes, offering up to heaven, no doubt, the sufferings it was inflicting on them.

Finally, at three o'clock, as they were crossing an interminable plain, without a single village in sight, Butterball quickly bent down and took out from under the coach seat a wide basket covered with a white cloth.

She took out of it first a little china plate, a slender silver cup, then a huge earthenware vessel in which two whole chickens, all ready sliced, had been preserved in their jelly; and many other things could be seen wrapped up in the basket: pâtés, fruits, titbits – she had packed enough provisions for a three-day journey so that she would not have to rely on the kitchens of the inns. The necks of four bottles peeped out from between the parcels of food. She picked up a chicken wing and, delicately, started to eat it, with one of those small light loaves called 'Régence' in Normandy.

All eyes were on her. Then the odour spread, causing nostrils to flare, bringing to everyone's mouth a flood of saliva accompanied by a painful contraction of the jaw under the ears. The contempt of the ladies for this whore grew fierce, like a longing to kill her, or to throw her out of the coach into the snow – her, her little cup, her basket and her provisions.

But Loiseau was devouring with his eyes the earthenware dish containing the chicken. He said, 'Madame has taken wise precautions, unlike us – good for her! There are some people who always manage to think of everything.'

She looked up at him.

'Would you like some, Monsieur? It's hard when you haven't had anything to eat all morning.'

He bowed.

'Good heavens, quite frankly I won't say no; I can't hold out any longer. All's fair in love and war, don't you think, Madame?'

And casting a look around, he added, 'At times like this, it's a real pleasure to find people who'll help you out.'

He had a newspaper, which he spread out so as not to stain his trousers, and using the point of a knife he always kept tucked into his pocket, he picked out a thigh nicely coated with jelly, tore it apart with his teeth, then chewed it with such evident satisfaction that a heavy sigh of distress spread through the coach.

But Butterball, with a humble, gentle voice, suggested to the nuns that they share her light meal. They both accepted like a shot, and, without lifting their eyes, started to eat as fast as they could, after stammering out their thanks. Cornudet too did not turn down his neighbour's offer, and they formed with the nuns a sort of table by spreading out newspapers across their knees.

Their mouths opened and closed without cease, swallowing, chomping, gobbling it all down ferociously. Loiseau, in his corner, was going at his food hammer and tongs, and in low tones he encouraged his wife to imitate him. For a long time she resisted the temptation, but, after a tense quiver in the pit of her stomach, she finally gave in. Then her husband, suddenly waxing eloquent, asked their 'charming companion' whether she would allow him to offer a little morsel to Mme Loiseau. She said, 'But of course, Monsieur,' with a friendly smile, and held out the earthenware dish.

An embarrassing moment occurred when they had uncorked the first bottle of Bordeaux; there was only one small cup. They passed it round, each one wiping the rim in turn. Cornudet alone, out of gallantry no doubt, set his lips to the place that was still moist from the mouth of the woman next to him.

Then, surrounded on all sides by people eating, and suffocated by the odours emanating from the food, the Count and Countess de Bréville, as well as M. and Mme Carré-Lamadon, started to suffer that hateful torment which still bears the name of Tantalus. All at once the factory owner's young wife emitted a sigh which made everyone look round; she was as white as the snow outside; her eyes closed, her head fell forward: she had fainted. Her husband, in a panic, implored everyone to help. They were all losing their heads, when the older of the two nuns, holding up the sick woman's head, slipped between her lips Butterball's little cup and made her swallow a few drops of wine. The pretty young lady stirred, opened her eyes, smiled and declared with a dying voice that she now felt perfectly well. But so that the same thing did not happen all over again, the nun forced her to drink a whole glass of Bordeaux, and added, 'It's just hunger, that's all.'

Then Butterball, blushing with embarrassment, looked at the four travellers who had still not broken their fast, and said with a stammer, 'Good Lord, if I might make so bold as to offer these ladies and gentlemen...' She fell silent, afraid of provoking scandal. Loiseau broke in, 'Oh for goodness' sake, in cases like this all men are brothers and must help each other out. Come on, ladies, don't stand on ceremony; accept, devil take it! Do we even know if we'll find a house to spend the night in? At the rate we're going, we won't reach Tostes before noon tomorrow.' They hesitated, nobody daring to take responsibility for saying yes.

But the Count resolved the matter. He turned round to the fat girl sitting there all intimidated, and putting on his gentlemanly airs, said to her, 'We are grateful to accept, Madame.'

The ice had been broken, and from now on it was all so much easier. Once the Rubicon had been crossed, they all

19

tucked in. The basket was emptied. It still contained a pâté de foie gras, a lark pâté, a piece of smoked tongue, some Crassane pears, a slab of Pont-l'Evêque cheese, some petits fours and a big jar full of gherkins and onions in vinegar, for Butterball, like all women, loved crudités.

They could hardly eat the young hussy's provisions without talking to her. So they started to make conversation, reservedly at first, then, as she kept her end up very well, they let themselves go a bit more. Mmes de Bréville and Carré-Lamadon, who were women of tact and refinement, put on a delicate and gracious air. The Countess in particular showed that amiable condescension of very noble ladies who can rub shoulders with anyone and still emerge unsullied, and she was charming. But sturdy Mme Loiseau, who had the soul of a gendarme, remained sour-faced, speaking little and eating a great deal.

Naturally they discussed the war. They recounted the horrible deeds done by the Prussians, and the brave exploits of the French; and all these people who were busy taking flight paid homage to the courage of other people. Soon personal anecdotes started to flow, and Butterball told them, with real feeling and that warmth of expression that women of the street sometimes have when conveying their natural upsurges of emotion, how she had left Rouen.

'I thought at first I'd be able to stay,' she said. 'I had a house full of things to eat, and I preferred to feed a few soldiers rather than go into exile heaven knows where. But when I saw those Prussians, I was quite simply knocked over! They made my heart swell with rage, and I spent the whole day weeping for shame. Oh, if only I were a man! I watched them from my window, those big fat pigs with their pointed helmets, and my maid had to hold my hands tight to stop me throwing my furniture down on them. Then some of them came to lodge in my house, so I jumped at the throat of the first one. They're no more difficult to strangle than anyone else! And I'd really have finished him off, if they hadn't dragged me away by the hair. I had to go into hiding after that. Anyway, as soon as I had a chance, I left, and here I am.'

They congratulated her warmly. She was growing in the esteem of her companions, who had not shown such boldness; and Cornudet, as he listened to her, continued to wear an approving and benevolent smile like that of an apostle; it was much as a priest might hear a devout parishioner praising God, for long-bearded democrats have a monopoly on patriotism just as men of the cloth have a monopoly on religion. He in turn spoke in doctrinaire tones, with the pompous weightiness he had learnt from the proclamations that were stuck up on the walls each day, and he ended up with a display of eloquence in which he magisterially laid into 'that scoundrelly Badinguet'[3].

But this immediately made Butterball angry for she was a Bonapartist. She went more red in the face than a ripe cherry and, stuttering with indignation, exclaimed, 'I'd like to have seen the rest of you in his place! Now that *would* have been a pretty pickle! *You're* the ones who betrayed him! There'd be nothing left but to leave France if we were governed by good-for-nothings like you!'

Cornudet, impassive, kept his disdainful, superior smile, but everyone sensed that coarse insults were about to start flying, when the Count stepped in and managed, not without difficulty, to calm down the exasperated girl, proclaiming in authoritative tones that all sincerely-held opinions were worthy of respect. However, the Countess and the wife of the factory owner, who harboured in their souls the irrational fear all decent people harboured towards the idea of a republic, and that instinctive affection that all women nurse towards flashy, despotic governments, felt drawn in spite of themselves to this prostitute full of dignity, whose feelings so closely resembled theirs.

The basket was empty. The ten of them had got to the bottom of it without difficulty, regretting that it was not any bigger. The conversation continued for some time, somewhat more frigidly now that they had finished eating.

Night was falling, the darkness gradually deepened, and the cold, which they felt more now that they were digesting, made Butterball shiver, despite her fat. Then Mme de Bréville offered her her footwarmer, the fuel of which had been topped up several times, and Butterball immediately accepted, for her feet felt completely frozen. Mmes Carré-Lamadon and Loiseau gave theirs to the nuns.

The coach driver had lit his lamps. They cast a bright light onto the cloud of steam rising from the sweating cruppers of the wheel-horses, and on either side of the road they lit up the snow which seemed to unwind under their flickering gleam.

It was impossible to make out anything inside the coach, but all at once there was a slight scuffle between Butterball and Cornudet, and Loiseau, whose eye pierced through the darkness, thought he saw the bushy-bearded man suddenly pull away, as if he had been dealt a well-aimed, soundless punch.

Tiny flickers of flame appeared ahead on the road. It was Tostes. They had been on the move for eleven hours, which, with the four lots of two hours' rest allotted to the horses to draw breath and have their oats, made fourteen.[4] They entered the town, and stopped outside the Hôtel du Commerce.

The coach door opened! A well-known noise sent a shudder down the spines of all the passengers; the rattle of a sabre sheath bumping along the ground. Straight away, the voice of a German shouted something.

Although the coach had halted, nobody got out, as if they thought they would be massacred as they emerged. Then the driver appeared holding one of his lamps, which suddenly cast its rays right into the back of the coach where the two rows of frightened faces were gazing open-mouthed and wide-eyed with surprise and terror.

Next to the coach driver was standing, fully visible in the lamplight, a tall, extremely slim blond young man, strapped tightly into his uniform like a girl into her corset, and wearing askew his flat, waxed cap, which gave him the appearance of the lackey in an English hotel. His enormous moustache, with its long straight sweep, tapering down to a point on both sides until it formed a single blond strand, so slender that it was impossible to tell where it ended, seemed to weigh on the corners of his mouth and, pulling on his cheek, gave his lips a downward turn.

Speaking in French with an Alsatian accent, he requested the travellers to get out, saying stiffly, 'Vill you please to get out, Ladies und Chentlemen?'

The two nuns were the first to obey, with the docility of saintly girls used to doing as they were told. The Count and Countess were the next to appear, followed by the factory owner and his wife, then by Loiseau pushing his sturdy better half in front of him. As he set foot on the ground, he said to the officer, 'Good evening, Monsieur,' more out of prudence than politeness. The other, insolent like all men who are in complete control, stared at him without a reply.

Butterball and Cornudet, although they had been sitting next to the door, were the last to climb out, solemn and haughty in the face of the enemy. The big fat girl tried to master her feelings and keep calm; the 'democrat' kept coiling his long reddish beard with a tragic and slightly trembling hand. They were keen to preserve their dignity, realising that in this sort of encounter, everyone is to some extent a representative of their country; they were both equally revolted by the spinelessness of their companions – she tried to show she had more pride than the other, respectable women, while he, fully aware that it was up to him to set an example, preserved in his entire attitude the mission of resistance that he had embarked upon when he undertook to break up the roads.

They went into the vast kitchen of the inn, and the German, having asked to see the authorisation for departure signed by the general-in-chief, on which were written the names, particulars, and professions of each traveller, looked the entire group over at length, comparing each of them to the written description.

Then he said brusquely, 'Zat vill be all,' and disappeared.

They started to breathe again. They were still hungry; supper was ordered. It took half an hour to prepare it, and while two servant women made a show of getting it ready, the group went to look at their rooms. They were all in a long corridor which ended with a glazed door with a meaningful number[5].

Finally they were about to sit down at table when the innkeeper himself appeared. He had been a horse vendor, and was a big asthmatic man, who still had fits of wheezing and hoarseness, and whose larynx emitted a phlegmy cough. His father had bequeathed to him the name of Follenvie.

He asked, 'Mademoiselle Elisabeth Rousset?'

Butterball shuddered and turned round.

'That's me.'

24

'Mademoiselle, the Prussian officer wishes to speak to you immediately.'

'To me?'

'Yes, if you are indeed Mademoiselle Elisabeth Rousset.'

She looked disconcerted, reflected for a moment, than said bluntly, 'Maybe he does, but I won't go.'

There was a stir around her; everyone started arguing, trying to guess the cause behind this order. The Count came up and said, 'You are wrong, Madame; your refusal may bring considerable difficulties in its wake, not just for you, but for all your companions too. One should never resist those who are stronger. If you go, it will surely not mean you running into any danger; it's doubtless to do with some formality that has been neglected.'

Everyone joined their voices to his, they begged her, they urged her, they expostulated with her, and finally they convinced her; for they all feared the complications which might result from her stubborn refusal. At last she said, 'All right, but it's only for you that I'll do it!'

The Countess took her hand. 'And we are grateful to you for it.'

She went out. They waited for her to come back before sitting down to eat.

Everyone said how sorry they were that they had not been summoned instead of that violent and irascible girl, and they mentally prepared various platitudes to trot out in case they were called in turn.

But after ten minutes she reappeared, breathing heavily, red and flustered, exasperated. She was stuttering, 'Oh, the villain! The villain!'

They all crowded round to ask what had happened, but she said nothing; and as the Count persisted, she replied with great dignity, 'No, it's none of your business, I can't say a thing.'

They thereupon sat down to a tall soup tureen from which rose the appetising odour of cabbage. Despite the preceding alarm, the supper was a merry occasion. The cider was good, and the Loiseau couple as well as the nuns had some, as it was cheaper. The others asked for wine; Cornudet demanded beer. He had a particular way of uncorking the bottle, making the liquid foam, and contemplating it as he tilted his glass, which he then held up between the lamp and his eye so he could appreciate its colour. When he drank, his bushy beard, which had kept the traces of his favourite brew, seemed to bristle with affection; he would gaze down from the corner of his eyes so as not to lose sight of his beer mug, and he seemed to be fulfilling the sole function for which he had been born. He looked exactly as if he were drawing up in his mind a comparison and, as it were, an affinity between the two great passions which occupied his entire life: Pale Ale and Revolution; and it was quite true that he could not sample the one without thinking about the other.

M. and Mme Follenvie were dining at the far end of the table. The man, puffing and blowing like a locomotive with a leak, had too much congestion in his chest to be able to speak while he ate, but his wife never stopped talking. She recounted all the impressions she had felt at the arrival of the Prussians, what they did, what they said – cursing them first and foremost because they were costing her money, and secondly because she had two sons in the army. She addressed her remarks especially to the Countess, flattered to be talking with a lady of quality.

Then she lowered her voice to make some more delicate comments, and her husband interrupted her from time to time, saying, 'You'd do better to keep quiet, Madame Follenvie.' But she took no notice, and continued:

'Yes, Madame, those men do nothing but eat potatoes and pork, and then pork and potatoes. And you can't say they're clean. Oh no! They do their business everywhere, saving your presence. And if only you could see them drilling for hours and days on end: they're all out there, in a field, and it's forward march, and about turn, and right turn, and left turn. At least if they were cultivating the land, or working on the roads of their own country!... But far from it, Madame, those military types are no use to anyone! And the poor ordinary folk have to feed them and they're out there learning how to slaughter people! I'm just an old woman without any education, it's true, but when I see them knocking their constitutions into a cocked hat, stamping up and down, morning, noon and night, I say to myself, "When there are people making so many useful discoveries, why should others go out of their way to make a nuisance of themselves? Honestly, isn't it perfectly dreadful to kill people, whether they're Prussian, or English, or Polish, or French?" If you get your own back on someone who's done something against you, it's bad, 'cause you're caught and punished; but when they exterminate our lads as if they were game, with rifles, then *that's* all right, since they give medals to the one that wipes out the most – isn't that so? No, believe you me, *that* I'll never understand!'

Cornudet raised his voice:

'War is barbarous when a peaceful neighbour is attacked; it's a sacred duty when it's a matter of defending your fatherland.'

The old woman lowered her head.

'Yes, when you defend yourself it's another matter; but

shouldn't we really be killing all the kings who do it all just for fun?'

Cornudet's eye lit up.

'Bravo, citizen!' he said.

M. Carré-Lamadon was deep in thought. Although he was a great admirer of the illustrious captains in the army, this peasant woman's common sense made him dream of the opulent wealth that would be brought into the country by so many idle and thus wasteful bodies, so many forces that were being sustained unproductively, when they could be set to work on the great industrial labours that it will take centuries to complete.

Mme Loiseau, leaving her seat, went to speak in low tones to the innkeeper. The big man was laughing, coughing, spitting; his enormous belly was quivering with joy at his neighbour's jokes, and he bought six half hogsheads of Bordeaux from him, for the spring, once the Prussians had gone.

Hardly was supper over when, as they were all dropping with exhaustion, they went to bed.

However, Loiseau, who had been observing things attentively, put his wife to bed, then glued his ear and his eye in succession to the keyhole, in an attempt to discover what he called 'the mysteries of the corridor'.

After about an hour, he heard a rustling noise, quickly looked, and saw Butterball appearing even more podgy than before in a dressing-gown of blue cashmere, edged with white lace. She was holding a lighted candle and heading to the room with the jokey label at the far end of the corridor. But a door to the side half-opened and, when she returned after a few minutes, Cornudet, in braces, was following her. They spoke in low tones, then stopped. Butterball seemed to be vigorously barring entry to her room. Loiseau, unfortunately, could not hear the words, but eventually, as they started to raise their voices, he was able to catch something of what they were saying. Cornudet was energetically persisting. He was saying, 'Come on, you're being silly, what difference does it make to you?'

She seemed indignant and replied, 'No, my friend, there are times when that sort of thing just isn't done; and then, here, it would be shameful.'

He refused to understand, no doubt, and asked why. Then she flew into a rage, raising her voice even more:

'*Why?* You don't understand *why?* When there are Prussians in the house, maybe in the next room?'

He was silent. This patriotic sense of shame coming from a whore who refused to accept a man's caresses when the enemy was nearby must have awoken the faltering dignity in his heart, for, after merely embracing her, he padded stealthily back to his room.

Loiseau, quite aroused, left the keyhole, cut a caper in his room, tied on his knotted headscarf, lifted up the sheet under which lay the heavy carcass of his lady wife, and awoke her with a kiss, murmuring, 'D'you love me, sweetheart?'

Then the whole house became silent. But there soon rose, from an indeterminate direction which could be the cellar just as much as the attic, a powerful, monotonous, regular snoring, a muffled and prolonged noise, with rumblings like those of a boiler under pressure. M. Follenvie was asleep.

As they had decided they would leave at eight o'clock the next morning, everyone gathered in the kitchen; but the coach, its tilt roofed with snow, was standing alone in the middle of the yard, without horses and without a driver. They looked for him in the stables, in the forage, in the coach-houses. Then all the men resolved to scour the countryside, and they set off. They found themselves on the square, with the church in the background and, on either side, low-roofed houses in which Prussian soldiers were visible. The first they saw was peeling potatoes. The second, further on, was washing the barber's shop. Another, with a beard up to his eyes, was cuddling a small child in tears, dandling him on his knees and trying to quieten him down; and the strapping peasant women, whose men were with the 'army at war', were indicating in sign language to their obedient victors the work that had to be done: cutting wood, ladling the soup onto the bread, grinding the coffee; one of them was even washing the linen of his hostess, a completely lame old grandma.

The Count, in astonishment, questioned the beadle who was coming out of the presbytery. The old churchman replied:

'Oh, those ones are no trouble; they're not even Prussians, by the sound of it. They come from further away, I don't really know where; and they've all left a wife and children behind; war's no fun for them, you can be sure! I bet the women weep for their menfolk over there just as much as here; and they're in for as much of a hard time of it as our people are. Here, in any case, we're not too badly off for the time being, since they're not being a nuisance and they work as if they were in their own homes. You see, Monsieur, poor folks have to help each other out… It's the high and mighty that make war.'

Cornudet, indignant at the cordial mutual understanding that had been established between victors and vanquished, withdrew, preferring to closet himself in the inn. Loiseau made a joke: 'They're repopulating the place.' M. Carré-Lamadon made a solemn remark: 'They are making reparations.' But nobody could find the coachman. Eventually they came across him in the village café, sitting quietly at a table with the officer's adjutant. The Count accosted him.

'Hadn't we given you orders to harness the horses for eight o'clock?'

'Well, yes, but I've since been given other orders.'

'What orders?'

'Not to harness at all.'

'Who gave you these orders?'

'The Prussian commander, hang it all!'

'Why?'

'I haven't the slightest idea. Go and ask him. I'm forbidden to harness the horses, so I won't harness them. And that's that.'

'Did he tell you this himself?'

'No, Monsieur, it was the innkeeper who gave me the orders on his behalf.'

'When was that?'

'Yesterday evening, as I was going to bed.'

The three men returned, full of disquiet.

They asked to see M. Follenvie, but the servant-woman replied that Monsieur, because of his asthma, never got up before ten o'clock. He had even given strict instructions that he was not to be woken any earlier, except in case of fire.

They wanted to see the officer, but this was absolutely impossible, although he was lodging at the inn. M. Follenvie alone was authorised to speak to him on civilian matters. So they waited. The women went back up to their rooms, and kept themselves busy with this and that.

Cornudet settled down right next to the tall fireplace in the kitchen where there was a blazing fire. He asked for one of the little tables from the café to be brought to him, and a bottle of beer, and he drew on his pipe – which enjoyed among the democrats a prestige almost equal to his own, as if it had served the fatherland by serving Cornudet. It was a superb meerschaum, admirably seasoned, as black as its master's teeth, but sweet-smelling, nicely curved, gleaming, fitting snugly in his hand, and adding the final touch to his physiognomy. And he sat there motionless, his eyes sometimes staring into the flames of the hearth, sometimes gazing at the fine head of foam in his beer mug; and each time he had pulled on his beer, he drew his long slender fingers through his long greasy hair with a satisfied look on his face, as he sniffed at his moustache with its fringe of foam.

Loiseau, claiming he wanted to stretch his legs, went to sell off some of his wine to the local retailers. The Count and the factory owner started to talk politics. They set about prophesying the future of France. The one believed in the house of Orléans, the other in some unknown saviour, a hero who would reveal himself when things were in desperate straits: a du Guesclin[6], a Joan of Arc perhaps? Or another Napoleon I? Ah, if only the Prince Imperial weren't so young![7] Cornudet, as he listened to them, smiled like a man who knows what destiny is planning. His pipe filled the kitchen with its aroma.

As ten o'clock was striking, M. Follenvie appeared. They quickly questioned him, but he could merely repeat, two or three times over, without variant, these words:

'What the officer told me was: "Monsieur Follenvie, you will forbid the coach to be harnessed tomorrow for these travellers. I do not wish them to leave without my orders. You understand. That is all."'

Then they wanted to see the officer. The Count sent him his card, to which M. Carré-Lamadon added his name and all his titles. The Prussian sent back word that he would allow these two men to speak to him when he had had his lunch, at about one o'clock.

The ladies reappeared and everyone had a bite to eat, in spite of their anxiety. Butterball seemed ill and deeply troubled.

They were finishing the coffee when the adjutant came to fetch the gentlemen.

Loiseau accompanied the two of them, but as they tried to take Cornudet along with them so as to give greater solemnity to the proceedings, he declared with pride that he intended never to have anything to do with Germans; and he settled back down in front of the fireplace, asking for another bottle of beer.

The three men went up and were led into the finest room in the inn, where the officer received them, stretched out in an armchair, his feet on the mantelpiece, smoking a long porcelain pipe, and wrapped up in a flamboyant dressing-gown, no doubt stolen from the abandoned dwelling of some middle-class man with bad taste. He did not stand up, did not greet them, did not look at them. He was a magnificent specimen of the loutishness that comes naturally to the victorious soldier.

After a few moments he finally said, 'Vat do you vant?'

The Count spoke up. 'We want to leave, Monsieur.'

'No.'

'May I make so bold as to ask you for the cause of this refusal?'

'Becoss I do not vant it.'

'I will respectfully point out to you, Monsieur, that your general-in-chief has granted us permission to leave for Dieppe; and I do not think that we have done anything to deserve this harsh treatment from you.'

'I do not vant it… zat is all… You can leef me.'

Having bowed, the three of them withdrew.

The afternoon was awful. They could not in the least understand this German capriciousness; and the strangest ideas went round and round in their heads. They were all gathered in the kitchen, endlessly discussing the matter, imagining the most unlikely things. Perhaps there was a plan to keep them as hostages – but with what aim? Or else take them off as prisoners? Or, perhaps, demand a huge ransom from them? At this thought, they were seized by an intense panic. The richest of them were the most horror-stricken, seeing themselves already constrained, if they were going to save their own skins, to pour sackfuls of gold into the hands of this insolent soldier. They racked their brains to concoct plausible lies, conceal the extent of their wealth, and pass themselves off as poor, very poor men. Loiseau removed his watch chain and hid it in his pocket. The falling night increased their apprehensions. The lamp was lit and, as there were still hours to go before dinner, Mme Loiseau suggested a game of *trente-et-un*. It would take their minds off things. They accepted. Cornudet himself, having extinguished his pipe out of politeness, took part.

The Count shuffled the cards – dealt… Butterball got thirty-one straight away; and soon the interest they took in the game laid to rest the fear that was haunting every mind. But Cornudet noticed that the Loiseau couple were in cahoots, and cheating.

As they were about to sit down at table, M. Follenvie reappeared; and in his hoarse voice, he uttered these words: 'The Prussian officer asks whether Mademoiselle Elisabeth Rousset has changed her mind yet.'

Butterball remained erect and pale; then suddenly turning

crimson, she was so suffocated with rage that she could no longer speak. Finally she exploded: 'You can go and tell that slob, that bastard, that swine of a Prussian that I will never consent; you hear me? Never, never, never.'

The hefty innkeeper went out. Then Butterball was surrounded, questioned, urged by everyone to disclose the mystery behind her visit. At first she resisted: but soon her exasperation got the better of her. 'What does he want, you ask?... What does he want? He wants to sleep with me!' she cried. Nobody was shocked by the expression, so great was their indignation. Cornudet smashed his beer mug as he banged it violently down onto the table. There was a clamour of loud protest against that vile trooper, and anger swept through them; all were united in resistance, as if each of them had been asked to share in the sacrifice demanded of her. The Count declared in disgust that those people behaved like the barbarians of olden times. The women especially showed Butterball a lively and caressing commiseration. The nuns, who only appeared at mealtimes, had lowered their heads and said nothing.

Still, they had dinner as soon as their first outburst of indignation had calmed down; but they said little; they were thinking.

The ladies retired early, and the men, as they smoked, organised a game of écarté to which they summoned M. Follenvie, as they intended to question him by stealth so as to discover ways of overcoming the officer's resistance. But he was completely absorbed in his card-game, listened to nobody, and did not answer; he just kept repeating, 'On with the game, gentlemen, on with the game!' His concentration was so intense that he forgot to hawk and spit, which sometimes meant his chest emitted blasts as from an organ pipe. His wheezing lungs went up and down the scales of asthma, from the deep, solemn notes up to the shrill squeaky hoarseness of young cockerels trying to crow.

He even refused to go up to bed when his wife, who was dropping with sleep, came to fetch him. So she went off by herself, for she was 'a lark', always up with the sun, whereas her husband was 'a night owl', always ready to spend the night with friends. He shouted out to her, 'You can put my egg-nog in front of the fire,' and turned back to his game. When they saw they would never get a word more from him, they declared it was time to turn in, and they all went off to bed.

They again rose quite early the following morning, with a tremulous hope and a greater desire to be off and away, stricken with terror at the idea of the day they would have to spend in this horrid little inn.

Alas! The horses stayed in the stable, the coach driver was nowhere to be seen. Having nothing better to do, they went to take a stroll round the coach.

Breakfast was a gloomy affair; and a certain chilliness had set in towards Butterball, for they had all slept on it and were starting to change their minds. Now they were almost resentful at this girl for not slipping off in secret to see the Prussian and thus create a nice surprise for her companions when they woke up. What could have been simpler? And in any case, who'd have known it? She could have saved appearances by getting the officer to say that she had taken pity on their distress. For her, it was all of so little importance!

But no one was yet prepared to admit to these thoughts.

In the afternoon, as they were all dying of boredom, the Count suggested that they go for a walk around the village. Everyone wrapped up warm, and the little group set off, apart from Cornudet, who preferred to stay by the fireside, and the nuns, who spent their days in church or at the priest's home.

The cold, which was growing daily more intense, stung their noses and ears cruelly; their feet hurt so much that each step was painful; and when the countryside opened up before them, it appeared so dreadfully gloomy to them under that limitless whiteness that they all immediately turned back, their souls frozen and their hearts bitter.

The four women walked ahead, the three men followed on, a few steps behind.

Loiseau, who understood the situation, suddenly asked if 'that hussy' was going to make them stay much longer in a place like this. The Count, courteous as ever, said that they could not ask a woman to make such a painful sacrifice, and that the decision would have to come from her. M. Carré-Lamadon remarked that if the French were to make an offensive return via Dieppe, as they were said to be planning, the armies might join battle at Tostes. This reflection made the two other men anxious. 'What if we escaped on foot?' said Loiseau. The Count shrugged. 'You can't be serious. In this snow? With the women? In any case, they'd immediately come after us and catch us up in ten minutes, and we'd be brought back as prisoners at the mercy of the soldiers.' This was true; they fell silent.

The ladies started talking fashion; but a certain constraint seemed to have come between them.

Suddenly, at the end of the street, the officer appeared. Against the snow that blocked the horizon, he stood out distinctly like a giant wasp in uniform, walking with his knees apart in that gait particular to military men who are trying their utmost not to stain their immaculately waxed boots.

He bowed as he passed in front of the ladies, and stared disdainfully at the men who, in any case, standing on their dignity, refused to raise their hats, although Loiseau made a gesture as if he were about to touch his forelock.

Butterball had blushed to the ears; and the three married women were overwhelmed by feelings of deep humiliation at being encountered by this soldier in the company of this whore he had treated in so cavalier a fashion.

Then they talked about him, his bearing, his face. Mme Carré-Lamadon, who had known many officers and judged them from the point of view of a connoisseur, found him not bad at all; she even expressed the regret that he was not French, as he would have made a handsome hussar and all the women would certainly have doted on him.

Once they were back, they had no idea what to do next. A few sharp words were even exchanged, and on quite trivial matters. The dinner was silent, and soon over; then everyone went up to bed, hoping to sleep so as to kill time.

They came down the following day with tired faces and exasperation in their hearts. The women hardly spoke to Butterball.

A bell rang. It was for a baptism. The fat young woman had a child being brought up by peasants in Yvetot. She did not see him even once a year, and never spared him a thought; but the idea of the child about to be baptised filled her heart with a sudden violent affection for her own youngster, and she absolutely insisted on attending the ceremony.

As soon as she had gone, everyone exchanged glances, and then drew up the chairs together, sensing that it was high time to take a decision. Loiseau had an inspiration: in his opinion, they should suggest to the officer that he just keep Butterball, and let the others go.

M. Follenvie agreed to perform the errand, but he came back down almost immediately. The German, who knew human nature, had shown him the door. He intended to keep everyone there until his desires were satisfied.

Then the vulgar temperament of Mme Loiseau exploded. 'But we're not going to stay here until we die of old age! Since it's that slut's job to do what she does with any man who wants, I don't see she's got any right to turn down one rather than another. I ask you – she picked up everyone she could find in Rouen, even the coach drivers! Yes, Madame, the coach driver of the *préfecture*! I know all about it; he buys his wine from us. And today, when she could be getting us out of a tight corner, the snotty-nosed little hussy decides to put on airs and graces!… Well in my opinion, the officer's behaving very well about it. Perhaps he hasn't had any for quite a while; and there were three of us ladies here that he'd certainly have preferred. But instead, he's quite happy to take the woman that belongs to everyone. He respects married women. Just remember this: he's in charge. All he needed was to say, "I want," and he could have got his soldiers to take us by force.'

The two women shuddered slightly. The eyes of little Mme Carré-Lamadon were shining, and she was rather pale, as if she imagined that the officer was already taking her by force.

The men, who were standing apart talking things over, came up. Loiseau was enraged: he wanted to deliver 'that wretched girl', bound hand and foot, to the enemy. But the Count, the scion of three generations of ambassadors, and with all the bearing of a diplomat, urged cunning. 'We need to force her to make up her mind,' he said.

So they started to plot.

The women came together in a huddle, they lowered their voices, and the discussion became general, as everyone gave their opinion. In fact, it was all handled decorously. The ladies in particular invented the most delicate turns of phrase and charming subtleties of expression to say the most indecent things. A stranger would not have understood a word, so carefully did they observe the linguistic proprieties. But the thin glaze of modesty in which every woman of the world is coated merely covers the surface, and they came into their own in this risqué adventure, and enjoyed themselves to the full when it came to it, feeling altogether in their element, and pawing at love with the sensuality of a greedy chef preparing someone else's dinner.

Their cheerfulness started spontaneously to return, as they finally started to see the funny side of the story. The Count made some rather off-colour jokes, but he told them so well that they raised a smile. Loiseau in turn came out with some smuttier stories which offended nobody; and the thought brutally expressed by his wife was at the forefront of everyone's mind: 'Since it's that whore's job, why should she turn down *him* rather than anyone else?' Pretty little Mme Carré-Lamadon even seemed to think that if it was her, she would turn down anyone else rather than *him*.

They prepared the blockade at length, as if they were about to lay siege to a fortress. Everyone agreed on the role they were to play, the arguments they would rely on, the manoeuvres they would need to execute. They settled the plan of attack, the ruses they would employ, and the surprise assaults they would launch, to force that living citadel to receive the enemy into her walls.

Cornudet however stayed apart, refusing to have anything to do with the whole business.

They were all so deeply intent on their plans that they did not hear Butterball return. But the Count whispered 'Shhh,' and they all looked up. There she was. They suddenly fell silent and a certain embarrassment at first prevented them from speaking to her. The Countess, who had learnt more than the others how to be duplicitously agreeable from her experience in the salons, asked her, 'Did you have a good time at the baptism?'

The fat young woman, still filled with emotion, told them all about it: how people had looked, the way they had stood, and even what the church had been like. She added, 'It's nice to pray sometimes.'

Nonetheless, until lunch, the ladies contented themselves with being friendly towards her, to gain her trust and make her more docile to their advice.

Once they had sat down to table, they started to make their approaches. They began to talk vaguely about self-sacrifice. They cited ancient examples: Judith and Holofernes, and then, without any real reason, Lucretia with Sextus, and Cleopatra forcing all her enemy generals to sleep with her and reducing them to serve her as if they were slaves. Whereupon they spun out a completely fantastic history, concocted in the imaginations of those ignorant millionaires, in which the female citizens of Rome went to Capua to lull Hannibal to sleep in their arms, and his lieutenants with him, and whole phalanxes of mercenaries to boot. They cited all the women who have brought conquerors to a halt, made of their own bodies a battlefield, a means of dominating, a weapon; all who have vanquished with their heroic caresses hideous or hated men, and surrendered their chastity to vengeance, all in a spirit of self-sacrifice.

They even spoke in veiled terms of that Englishwoman of noble family who had allowed herself to be inoculated with a horrible contagious illness so as to infect Bonaparte, who was miraculously saved, by a sudden moment of weakness, just as the hour of the fateful rendezvous was striking.

And all this was narrated in a decent, moderate way, sometimes made livelier by a tone of enthusiasm designed to arouse emulation.

Anyone might have thought, in the end, that the only role of a woman in this world was a perpetual sacrifice of her person, a continual self-abandonment to the whims of the soldiery.

The two nuns seemed not to hear, being absorbed in deep meditation. Butterball said nothing.

For the whole afternoon they allowed her to think things over. But instead of calling her 'Madame' as they had until then, they simply addressed her as 'Mademoiselle', without anyone knowing quite why, as if they had wanted to take her down a peg or two from the esteem she had managed to earn, and make her feel how shameful her position was.

Just as the soup was being served, M. Follenvie reappeared, repeating the words he had said the day before. 'The Prussian officer asks whether Mademoiselle Elisabeth Rousset has changed her mind yet.'

Butterball retorted sharply, 'No, Monsieur.'

But at dinner the coalition weakened. Loiseau came out with three unfortunate turns of phrase. Everyone was racking their brains to think of new examples, but they could not find any. Then the Countess, without premeditation perhaps, but feeling a vague need to pay homage to Religion, questioned the older of the nuns about the great deeds in the lives of the saints. Now, many of them had committed acts which would in our eyes be crimes; but the Church doubtless absolves such misdeeds when they are performed for the greater glory of God, or for the good of one's neighbour. This was a powerful argument: the Countess turned it to her account. Then, either through one of those tacit understandings, those veiled complicities in which anyone who wears ecclesiastical habits excels, or simply through a happy lack of intelligence, a useful stupidity, the old nun added her formidable support to the conspiracy. They had thought she was timid, but she showed herself to be bold, verbose, violent. *She* was not troubled by the tentative gropings of casuistry; her doctrine seemed a rod of iron; her faith never hesitated; her conscience had not a single scruple. She found Abraham's sacrifice perfectly simple, for she would have killed mother and father straight away if given orders from on high; and nothing, in her view, could fail to be pleasing to the Lord when the intention behind it was praiseworthy. The Countess, making the most of the sacred authority of her unexpected accomplice, made her produce what amounted to an edifying paraphrase on that moral axiom: 'The end justifies the means.'

She continued to question her.

'And so, Sister, you think that God accepts all our good intentions, and forgives the deed when the motive is pure?'

'Who could doubt it, Madame? An action that is blameworthy in itself often becomes meritorious thanks to the thought that inspires it.'

And so they went on, unravelling God's designs, foreseeing his decisions, making out that he took an interest in things which, to tell the truth, barely concerned him.

All this was veiled, cunning, discreet. But every word uttered by the holy sister in her wimple made another breach in the courtesan's indignant resistance. Then, as the conversation went off at something of a tangent, the woman with the rosary talked about the houses of her order, about her mother superior, about herself, and her charming little neighbour, dear Sister Saint-Nicéphore. They had been asked to go to Le Havre to work in the hospitals looking after the hundreds of soldiers affected by smallpox. And she depicted those poor sick men, describing their illness in detail. And here they were, stopped en route by the whims of this Prussian; a great number of Frenchmen might be dying, when they could have saved them perhaps! It was her speciality, saving soldiers; she had been in the Crimea, in Italy, in Austria; and as she recounted her campaigns, she suddenly revealed herself to be one of those trumpet-and-drum nuns, seemingly made to be camp-followers and to pick up the wounded from the hurly-burly of battles and, more effectively than any commanding officer, to bring to heel strapping but undisciplined soldiers with a single word; a real 'Tantarara!' nun, whose ravaged face, pitted with countless pockmarks, seemed an image of the devastations of war.

Nobody uttered a word after she had finished; they thought she had created an excellent effect.

As soon as the meal was over, they quickly went up to their rooms, and came down the next morning quite late.

Breakfast was a tranquil affair. They were giving the seed sown the night before time to germinate and bear fruit.

The Countess suggested going for a walk in the afternoon; then the Count, as had been agreed, took the arm of Butterball, and remained behind the others, with her.

He talked to her in that familiar, paternal, somewhat disdainful tone which staid men use with women of the street, calling her 'my dear child', addressing her from the heights of his social position, his incontrovertible honour. He went straight away to the heart of the matter.

'So you prefer to leave us here, exposed like yourself to all the acts of violence that would follow a defeat of the Prussian troops, rather than to consent to one of those little deeds of kindness that you have so often performed in your life?'

Butterball did not reply.

He came at her with gentleness, with reason, with an appeal to sentiment. He managed to remain 'Monsieur le Comte', while at the same time stooping to flirtatious banter when necessary, full of compliments, amiable, in fact. He spoke in the highest terms of the service she would be doing them, spoke of their gratitude; then suddenly, addressing her cheerfully and familiarly, he exclaimed, 'You know what, my dear, he'd be able to boast of having enjoyed a pretty girl of a kind he won't often find in *his* country.'

Butterball did not reply and went to catch up with the others.

Once back at the inn, she went up to her room and did not reappear. Their anxiety was extreme. What was she going to do? If she resisted, what a pickle they'd be in!

The hour struck for dinner; they waited for her in vain. M. Follenvie came in and announced that Mlle Rousset was feeling unwell, and that they could start their meal. They all pricked up their ears. The Count went up to the innkeeper and said, in a low voice, 'All fixed?'

'Yes.'

Observing the proprieties, he said nothing to his companions, but simply gave them a quick nod. Immediately a great sigh of relief was heaved from every chest, and their faces brightened up considerably. Loiseau cried, 'Good heavens! The champagne is on me, if there's any to be found in this establishment'; and Mme Loiseau was disquieted when the proprietor returned with four bottles in his hands. Everyone had suddenly become communicative and noisy; a ribald merriment filled every heart. The Count seemed to notice that Mme Carré-Lamadon was charming, the factory owner paid compliments to the Countess. The conversation was lively, playful, full of witticisms.

Suddenly, Loiseau, his face anxious and lifting his arms up, bellowed, 'Quiet!' Everyone immediately fell silent, surprised and almost panic-stricken. Then he strained his ears to listen, motioned with his hands to say 'Shhh!', raised his eyes to the ceiling, listened again, and then resumed, in his natural voice, 'Don't worry, everything's all right.'

They struggled to understand, but soon a smile crossed every face.

After a quarter of an hour he started the same joke all over, repeating it several times in the course of the evening; and he kept pretending to be shouting up to someone in the storey above, giving him bits of advice full of double entendres, drawing on all the wit of a travelling salesman. At times he would strike a sad and solemn pose to sigh, 'Poor lass'; or else he would murmur between clenched teeth, with an expression of rage, 'Go on, you beggarly Prussian!' Sometimes, when they were least expecting it, he would repeatedly cry in vibrant tones, 'Enough! Enough!' adding, as if talking to himself, 'So long as we get to see her again; I hope he doesn't kill her, wretched man!'

Although these jokes were in deplorable taste, they amused everyone and offended no one, for indignation is dependent on social milieu as much as everything else, and the atmosphere that had little by little developed around them was thick with licentious ideas.

At dessert, the women themselves made witty and discreet allusions. Every eye gleamed; they'd had a lot to drink. The Count, who even when he let himself go a little maintained an appearance of great gravity, came up with a highly enjoyable comparison between the end of the winter season at the pole and the joy of shipwrecked men who see a route to the south opening up before them.

Loiseau, his tongue set wagging, stood up with a glass of champagne in his hand. 'I drink to our deliverance!' Everyone was on their feet; they acclaimed him. The two nuns themselves, urged on by the ladies, consented to take a tiny sip of this sparkling wine they had never tasted. They declared it was like fizzy lemonade, although more refined.

Loiseau summed up the situation.

'It's a great shame we don't have a piano because we could strike up a quadrille!'

Cornudet had not said a word, not made a move; he even seemed to be absorbed in the most serious thoughts, and sometimes, with a furious gesture, he would draw on his great beard as if he wanted to pull it out even longer. Finally, around midnight, as the party was about to break up, Loiseau, swaying on his feet, suddenly gave him a light punch in the stomach and jabbered to him, 'You're not exactly a barrel of laughs this evening; got nothing to say, citizen?' But Cornudet looked up suddenly, and stared round at the group with eyes bright with anger.

'Let me tell the whole lot of you that what you've just done is absolutely vile!'

He stood up, went to the door, repeated, 'Absolutely vile!' and vanished.

This at first cast a pall on the proceedings. Loiseau, completely taken aback, stood there dumbstruck; but he soon regained his composure and suddenly, creased with laughter, started to repeat, 'Sour grapes! Talk about sour grapes!' As no one understood, he told them about the 'mysteries of the corridor'. Then there was a formidable outburst of renewed gaiety. The ladies were overcome by hilarity. The Count and M. Carré-Lamadon laughed till they cried. They couldn't believe it.

'What? You're sure? He wanted to…'

'I saw it, I tell you.'

'And she turned him down…'

'Because the Prussian was in the room next door.'

'You've got to be joking.'

'I swear it.'

The Count was choking with laughter. The factory owner was holding his hands to his belly. Loiseau continued:

'And now you can see why this evening he didn't find the joke funny at all, no, not in the slightest.'

And all three went off again, aching and breathless.

Thereupon they separated. But Mme Loiseau, who was easily nettled, remarked to her husband as they were getting into bed, that little Mme Carré-Lamadon, that 'old bag', had been forcing herself to smile all evening. 'You know, when women get the hots for a uniform, whether it's French or Prussian, good heavens, they don't mind in the slightest!… My God, but it's sad!'

And all night long, in the darkness of the corridor, there could be heard a continual to and fro of rustles, faint and barely audible noises like that of light breathing, the scampering of bare feet, imperceptible creakings. And of course it was quite a while before they got to sleep, for streaks of light shone for a long time beneath their doors. Champagne has that effect; it disturbs your sleep, so they say.

The next day, a clear winter sun made the snow gleam dazzlingly. The coach, finally harnessed, was waiting in front of the door, while an army of white pigeons, strutting around in their thick feathers, their pink eyes with a black dot in the middle agleam, were gravely promenading between the legs of the six horses, and pecking for food in the steaming dung that they scattered.

The coachman, enveloped in his sheepskin coat, was smoking a pipe on his seat, and all the travellers, radiant with relief, were rapidly having provisions wrapped up for the rest of the journey.

The only one they were still waiting for was Butterball. She appeared.

She seemed a little troubled and ashamed; and she advanced timidly towards her companions who all, with one movement, turned away as if they had not seen her. The Count took his wife's arm with a dignified air and led her away from this impure contact.

The fat young woman stopped in stupefaction; then, summoning up all her courage, she went up to the factory owner's wife, humbly murmuring 'Good day, Madame.' The other merely nodded curtly and impertinently, accompanying her gesture with a stare of outraged virtue. Everyone seemed tremendously busy, and they kept their distance from her as if she had been transporting an infectious disease in her skirts. Then they hurried over to the coach where she was the last to arrive, all alone, taking in silence the seat she had occupied during the first half of the route.

They seemed not to see her, not to know her; but Mme Loiseau, considering her distantly, said in indignant half-tones to her husband, 'A good thing I don't have to sit next to her.'

The heavy carriage shook, and the journey recommenced.

At first nobody spoke. Butterball did not dare to lift her eyes. She felt at one and the same time indignant at all her fellow-travellers, and humiliated at having yielded, soiled by the kisses of that Prussian into whose arms they had hypocritically flung her.

But the Countess, turning to Mme Carré-Lamadon, soon broke this painful silence.

'I believe you know Mme d'Etrelles?'

'Yes indeed, she's a friend of mine.'

'She's a charming woman!'

'Delightful! A really high-class person, very well educated too, and an artist to her fingertips; she sings delightfully well, and draws to perfection.'

The factory owner was chatting to the Count, and in the midst of the clatter of the windows a word sometimes became audible: 'Coupon… falls due… premium… settlement…'

Loiseau, who had swiped the old pack of cards from the inn, greasy as it was from five years' contact with the dirty unwiped tables, launched into a game of bezique with his wife.

The nuns took from their belts the long rosaries hanging there, and together made the sign of the cross; and all at once their lips began to move quickly, getting faster and faster, forcing the pace of their indistinct murmur as if competing to see who could recite the *Oremus* most often; and from time to time they would kiss a medal, make the sign of the cross again, and then recommence their rapid and continual mumblings.

Cornudet was reflecting, motionless.

After three hours on the road, Loiseau gathered up his cards. 'I'm hungry,' he said.

Then his wife took out a parcel tied up with string from which she brought out a piece of cold veal. She cut it neatly into thin, firm slices, and both of them set to.

'What about doing the same?' said the Countess. They agreed, and she unwrapped the provisions prepared for the two married couples. There was, in one of those long jars with a china hare on the lid to indicate that *lièvre en pâté* is contained within, a succulent selection of meats in which white rivers of fat trickled through the brown flesh of the game, mixed together with other finely minced meat. A nice slab of Gruyère, wrapped in a newspaper, still had the words 'News in Brief' imprinted on its smooth sticky surface.

The two nuns took out a slice of sausage smelling of garlic; and Cornudet, digging deep into both of the vast pockets of his short sackcloth coat, pulled out of one four hard-boiled eggs and from another the heel of a loaf. He detached the shell, tossed it into the straw at his feet, and started to bite into the eggs, letting bright yellow specks fall onto his big bushy beard, where they seemed to shine like stars.

Butterball, in the haste and turmoil of getting up, had not had time to think of anything; and she stared, exasperated and choking with anger, at all those people placidly eating. At first, a tumultuous rage made her tense up, and she opened her mouth as if to pour out the stream of insults rising to her lips at their disgraceful behaviour; but she was unable to speak, choked as she was by frustration.

Nobody spared her a glance or a thought. She felt drowned in the contempt of those oh-so-respectable rascals who had first sacrificed her and then cast her aside, like some unclean, useless object. Then she thought of her basket, crammed with all the good things they had greedily devoured: her two chickens glistening with jelly, her pâtés, her pears, her four bottles of Bordeaux; and her fury suddenly subsided, like a cord pulled too taut and suddenly snapping, and she felt on the verge of tears. She made a terrific effort, stiffening and swallowing her sobs as children do, but her tears rose, shining on the rim of her eyes, and soon two big fat drops fell from her eyes and trickled slowly down her cheeks. Others followed them more rapidly, running down like drops of water filtering through a rock, and falling regularly on the plump curve of her bosom. She remained bolt upright, staring in front of her, her face pale and rigid, hoping no one would see her.

But the Countess noticed and alerted her husband with a gesture. He shrugged, as if to say, 'Well? It's not my fault.' Mme Loiseau uttered a mute laugh of triumph and murmured, 'She's crying for shame.'

The two nuns had resumed their prayers, having rolled the remnants of their sausage up in a piece of paper.

Then Cornudet, busy digesting his eggs, stretched his long legs out on the seat opposite, threw himself back, folded his arms, smiled like a man who has just thought of a good trick to play, and started to whistle the Marseillaise.[8]

Everyone's face darkened. The people's song, it was obvious, was not to the liking of his fellow-travellers. They turned edgy and irritable, and seemed ready to start howling, like dogs when they hear a hurdy-gurdy. He noticed this; now there was no stopping him. Sometimes he even hummed the words:

'*Oh sacred love of fatherland,*
Our vengeful arms lead and sustain!
Belovèd freedom, join your strength
To your defenders, might and main!'

They sped along more quickly, as the snow had hardened: and all the way to Dieppe, during the long grey and gloomy hours of the journey, as the coach bounced along, and night fell, and then in the pitch darkness of the coach, he kept up, with a ferocious obstinacy, his vengeful and monotonous whistling, forcing his weary and exasperated fellow-travellers to listen to the song from beginning to end, and to remember each word and fit it to the right note.

And Butterball carried on crying; and sometimes a sob that she had been unable to hold back escaped, in the pause between two verses, into the dark.

The Confession

The noonday sun is pouring down all across the fields. They spread out, swelling gently, between the clumps of trees on the farms; and the various crops, the ripened rye and the yellowing corn, the light green oats, the dark green clover, drape their great mantle, striped and gently waving, over the bare belly of the earth.

Over in the distance, at the top of a swell of ground, lined up like soldiers, an interminable line of cows, some of them lying down, the others standing, blinking their big eyes in the blazing sunlight, are ruminating and grazing in a field of clover as wide as a lake.

And two women, mother and daughter, walk along, their hips swaying gently, one in front of the other, through a narrow path cut through the crops, towards that regiment of cattle.

Each of them is carrying two zinc buckets held out from their bodies by the hoop of a barrel; and from the metal of the bucket, at every step they take, there flashes a white, dazzling flame, a reflection of the sun blazing down on it.

They are not speaking. They are going to milk the cows. They arrive, set a bucket on the ground, and go up to the two closest cows, which they force to their feet with a kick in the ribs from their clogs. The animal rises, slowly, on its forelegs first, and then, with more of an effort, lifts its broad crupper, which seems weighed down by the enormous dug of blond, pendulous flesh.

And the two Malivoires, mother and daughter, on their knees under the cow's belly, pull with a rapid movement of their hands on the swollen udder, which at every tug squirts a thin stream of milk into the bucket. The yellowish foam rises up to the rim and the women go from beast to beast until they reach the end of the long line.

As soon as they have finished milking one cow, they push it away, so it can graze on a still untouched stretch of greenery.

Then they set off home, more slowly, weighed down by the milk, the mother in front, the daughter behind.

But the daughter suddenly stops, sets down her burden, sits down and bursts into tears.

Mother Malivoire, no longer hearing the sound of her steps, turns round and stands there looking dumbstruck.

'What'z up?' she says.

And the daughter, Céleste, a big redhead with burnt hair, and burnt cheeks with freckles as if drops of fire had fallen onto her face when she was labouring out in the sun one day, murmured with a low groan like that of a beaten child:

'Oi just can't carry me milk!'

Her mother looked at her suspiciously. She repeated:

'What'z up?'

Céleste repeated, sitting flopped down between her two buckets, and hiding her eyes with her apron:

'It'z weighin' me down. Oi just can't.'

Her mother, for the third time, repeated:

'What'z up?'

And her daughter groaned:

'Oi think I muz' be in the fam'ly way.'

And she started sobbing.

The old woman in turn laid down her burden, so thunderstruck that she could think of nothing to say. Finally she stammered:

'Yur... yur in the fam'ly way, now, are yer? You really think yer moight be?'

The Malivoires were rich farmers, well-to-do, serious,

respected, cunning and strong.

Céleste stammered:

'Oi think zo, yeh… Oi muz' be.'

The horror-stricken mother gazed at her daughter sitting all downcast and teary-eyed in front of her. After a few seconds she cried:

'In the fam'ly way! Yur in the fam'ly way! How'd that happen to yer, yer liddle 'uzzy?'

And Céleste, shaken with emotion, murmured:

'Oi think as it muzd 'ave bin in Polyte's cart.'

The old woman racked her brains trying to understand, trying to guess, trying to know who could have done such a thing to her daughter. If it was a wealthy, respectable lad, they might come to some arrangement. It wouldn't be a complete catastrophe; Céleste wasn't the first girl something like this had happened to; but it vexed her all the same, considering the way people talk and the position they were in.

She resumed:

'An' 'oo was it as did that to yer, yer liddle slut?'

And Céleste, resolved to say everything, stammered:

'Oi think as it muzd 'ave bin Polyte.'

Then Mother Malivoire, out of her mind with rage, flung herself on her daughter and started to beat her so frantically that she lost her bonnet.

She lashed out with her fists, on her head, her back, everywhere; and Céleste, spread out lengthwise between the two buckets, which afforded her some protection, merely hid her face in her hands.

All the cows had stopped grazing in surprise, and had turned round to gaze with their big eyes. The last of them mooed, her muzzle stretched out towards the women.

After having administered such a drubbing that she

was quite out of breath, Mother Malivoire, panting heavily, stopped; and coming to her senses a little, she decided to look the situation fully in the face:

'Polyte! God A'mighdy, to think it'z 'im! 'Ow could yer, with a coach driver! Lost yer bloomin' mind 'ave yer? 'E muzd 'ave put a spell on yer, that's for certain, a good-fer-nothin' loike that!'

And Céleste, still lying full length, murmured into the dust: ''E give me a free roide!'

And then the old Norman woman understood.

Every week, on Wednesdays and Saturdays, Céleste would go to take into town the products of the farm: poultry, cream and eggs.

She would set off at seven o'clock with her two huge baskets on her arms, dairy products in one, hens in the other; and she would go to wait on the highway for the Yvetot coach.

She set her merchandise on the ground and sat in the ditch, while the hens with their stubby, pointed beaks, and the ducks with their broad, flat beaks, sticking their heads out from between the wickerwork bars, gazed out with their stupid, round, surprised eyes.

Soon the old boneshaker, a kind of yellow box topped by a cap of black leather, came along, shaking its backside to the jerky clip-clop of a white nag.

And Polyte, the coachman, a big merry-faced lad, already with a paunch though still young, and so cooked by the sun, burnt by the wind, drenched by the showers, and steeped in aquavit that his face and neck were the colour of brick, shouted from the distance as he cracked his whip:

'Good day there, Miss Céleste! And 'ow'z your 'ealth and temper?'

She held out to him, one after the other, her baskets, which he stowed away on the top of the vehicle; then she would climb up, lifting her leg high to reach the footboard, showing her sturdy calf with its blue stocking.

And each time, Polyte would repeat the same joke: 'Well well, blezz my 'eart, *that* 'asn't grown any slimmer!'

And she would laugh, finding his remark funny.

Then he would utter a 'Gee up, Lassy!' which set his skinny horse on its way again. Then Céleste, reaching for her purse in the depths of her pocket, slowly took out ten sous, six sous for her and four for the baskets, and passed them to Polyte over his shoulder. He would take them, saying:

'So today's not the day we're goin' to 'ave our bit o' fun then?'

And he laughed to his heart's content as he turned round to contemplate her at his ease.

It cost her a lot to have to pay this half franc each time for a journey of three kilometres. And when she didn't have the change, she suffered all the more, being unable to bring herself to fork out a whole coin.

And one day, when it was time to pay, she asked:

'Fer a good fare like me, you could just take six sous, couldn't yer?'

He started to laugh:

'Six sous, moy sweed'eart? You're worth more 'n that, and that's fer sure.'

She persisted:

'That would mean a good two francs a month for yer.'

He cried, with a flick of his whip across his nag:

'Look 'ere, oi'm an easy-goin' feller, oi'll let yer off if we can 'ave a bit o' fun.'

She asked, naively:

'What yer sayin'?'

He was enjoying himself so much he was spluttering with laughter.

'A bit o' fun is a bit o' fun, loike. A bit o' fun with a boy an' a girl, two steps forward, no need fer a band.'

She understood, blushed, and declared:

'Oi don't go in fer that koind o' game, Master Polyte.'

But he didn't lose heart and repeated, enjoying himself more and more:

'You'll come round to it, moy sweed'eart, a bit o' fun for a boy an' a girl!'

And ever since then, each time she paid him he had got into the habit of saying:

'So today's not the day we're going to 'ave our bit o' fun then?'

Now she too joked about it, and replied:

'Not today, Master Polyte, but Zaterday, and that's a promise!'

And he would exclaim, still with a smile:

'Agreed, then: Zaterday it is, moy sweed'eart!'

But she mentally calculated that, since all this had been going on for two years, she had paid forty-eight francs to Polyte, and you don't find forty-eight francs hanging from trees, out here in the countryside; and she also calculated that, in another two years, she would have paid nearly a hundred francs.

So one day, one spring day when they were alone, as he was asking as he always did, 'So today's not the day we're going to 'ave our bit o' fun then?' she replied:

'As yer please, Master Polyte.'

He wasn't in the least bit surprised and straddled the rear seat murmuring with a contented expression:

'That's the way. Oi knew as yer'd come round.'

And the old white horse started to trot so gently that it seemed to be dancing on the spot, deaf to the voice that sometimes cried from the inside of the vehicle, 'Gee up, Lassy! Gee up, Lassy!'

Three months later Céleste realised she was pregnant.

She had recounted all this in a tearful voice to her mother. And the old woman, pale with fury, said:

'So 'ow much did it cost, then?'

Céleste replied:

'Four months, that makes eight francs, dunnit.'

Then the rage of the peasant woman knew no bounds, and she flung herself back on her daughter, and beat her all over again until she ran out of breath. Then she picked herself up and said:

'Did you tell 'im as you was pregnant?'

'No, o' course I dain't.'

'And why dain't yer?'

'Cos 'e moighd 'ave started askin' me to start payin' again!'

And the old woman reflected. Then, picking up her buckets:

'Come on then, get up, an' try an' get a move on.'

Then, after a pause, she said:

'An' doahn' go tellin' im until 'e stardz to notice; that way we can zave on six or eight months!'

And Céleste, having hauled herself to her feet, still crying, her hair all dishevelled and her face swollen, set off again with a heavy gait, murmuring:

'*Course* I won't tell 'im!'

First Snow

The long promenade of la Croisette curves along the edge of the blue waves. Over there, on the right, the Esterel projects far out to sea. It bars the view, blocking the horizon with its attractive southern setting, a series of peaked and strangely shaped summits.

On the left, the islands of Sainte-Marguerite and Saint-Honorat, reclining in the water, show off their backs covered with pine trees.

And all along the wide gulf, all along the high mountains that are grouped around Cannes, the white populace of the villas seems to be sleeping in the sun. You can see them in the distance, the shining houses, scattered from top to bottom of the mountains like patches of snow against the dark green vegetation.

Those closest to the water open their gates onto the vast promenade bathed by the tranquil waves. The weather is fine and mild. It is a nice warm winter's day, with just the slightest fresh breeze. Above the seas of gardens, orange trees and lemon trees hanging with golden fruits are visible. Ladies walk slowly down the sandy garden paths, followed by children bowling hoops; or else they chat with gentlemen.

A young woman has just come out of her neat, pretty little house, with its front door on la Croisette. She pauses for a moment to look at the people out for a stroll, smiles, and with the slow gait of someone quite worn out, makes for an empty bench facing the sea. Weary already after only twenty paces, she sits down, breathing heavily. Her pale face seems that of a dead woman. She coughs, and brings up to her lips her transparent fingers, as if to control the shaking of her body that so exhausts her.

She looks at the sky filled with its sunshine and its swallows, the capricious summits of the Esterel in the distance and, right nearby, the sea so blue, so calm, so lovely.

She smiles again, and murmurs:

'Oh, how happy I am!'

And yet she knows that she is dying, that she won't see the spring, that, in a year's time, along this same promenade, these same people passing by in front of her will be back to breathe in the warm air of this gentle country, with their children grown a little taller, with their hearts still filled with hope, affection, and happiness, while within an oak coffin the poor flesh that still remains to her today will have rotted away, leaving nothing but bones lying there in the silken dress she has chosen for a shroud.

She will exist no more. All the things of life will continue for others. It will be all over for her, all over for good. She will exist no more. She smiles, and breathes, as deep as she can with her sickly lungs, the aromatic odours coming from the gardens.

And she starts to dream.

She remembers. She was married off, four years ago now, to a Norman gentleman. He was a sturdy, bearded fellow, high in colour, broad-shouldered, short on intelligence and always merry and cheerful.

They were made to tie the knot for financial reasons that she never learnt of. She would have been happy to say 'no'. She nodded 'yes', so as not to vex her mother and father. She was a Parisian girl, light-hearted and full of the joy of life.

Her husband took her to his château in Normandy. It was a

huge stone building surrounded by tall, ancient trees. A clump of pines stretched up and closed off the view. On the right, a gap opened out onto the plain which spread out in its emptiness as far as the distant farms. A side road went past the gate and led to the main road, three kilometres away.

Oh, she remembered it all! Her arrival, her first day in her new home, and her lonely life after that.

When she climbed out of the carriage, she looked at the old building and declared with a laugh:

'It's not very cheerful!'

Her husband started to laugh in turn and replied:

'Pooh! You get used to it! You'll see. *I* never get bored here.'

That day they spent a long time hugging and kissing, and she didn't find that the time dragged. The next day they did the same again, and the whole week, to tell the truth, was consumed by caresses.

Then she busied herself with organising the inside of the house. That took a good month. The days went by, one after the other, in trivial and yet absorbing occupations. She was learning the value and the importance of the little things of life. She learnt that it is possible to take an interest in the price of eggs, which cost a few centimes more or less depending on the season.

It was summer. She would go out into the fields to watch them harvesting. The cheerful sunshine kept her heart cheerful too.

Autumn came. Her husband started to go out hunting. He would leave in the morning with his two dogs Médor and Mirza. Then she would be left alone, without, however, feeling Henry's absence. She loved him dearly, of course, but she didn't miss him. When he came back, the dogs in particular absorbed her affections. She would look after them every evening with the tenderness of a mother, caressing them constantly, giving them a thousand charming little nicknames that it would never have entered her head to apply to her husband.

He would invariably tell her all about his day's hunting. He would describe the exact places where he had come upon the partridges; he would be amazed he hadn't found any hares among Joseph Ledentu's clover, or else would seem indignant at the behaviour of M. Lechapelier of Le Havre, who kept patrolling the boundary of his lands to shoot at the game that he, Henry de Parville, had started.

She would reply:

'Yes, really, that's not nice,' while her mind was on other things.

Winter came, the cold, rainy Normandy winter. The interminable showers fell on the slates of the great angular roof, pointing up as sharp as a blade towards the sky. The roads looked like rivers of mud; the countryside was one muddy plain; and nothing could be heard but the noise of falling water; nothing could be seen but the movement made by the whirling crows as they flew above like a cloud unfurling, dropped into a field, then headed off again.

At around four o'clock, an army of those dark winged creatures would come and perch in the big beech trees to the left of the château, uttering deafening cries. For nearly an hour, they would flutter from treetop to treetop, seeming to fight, cawing away and filling the greyish branches with the black flurry of their movement.

She would gaze at them every evening, heavy at heart, imbued with the mournful melancholy of night falling on the deserted lands.

Then she rang for the lamp to be brought, and sat closer to

the fire. She burnt piles of wood without managing to heat the vast rooms that had been invaded by the damp. And she was cold all day long, everywhere, in the living-room, at meals, in her bedroom. She was cold to the bone, she felt. Her husband would return only at dinner-time, for he was always out hunting, or else busy with the sowing, the ploughing, all the activities of the countryside.

He would return cheerful and mud-spattered, rubbing his hands and declaring:

'Bloody awful weather!'

Or:

'It's good to have a nice fire!'

Or he would sometimes ask:

'What have we got to say for ourselves today? Happy, are we?'

He was contented, healthy, free of desires, dreaming of nothing other than this simple, wholesome, tranquil life.

Around December, when the snows arrived, she suffered so terribly from the icy air in the château – that old château which seemed to have grown colder across the centuries just as human beings do across the years – that she asked her husband one evening:

'Henry, don't you think it would be a good idea for you to put a stove in here? It would drive the damp out of the walls. I simply cannot get warm, from morning to night.'

He was at first dumbfounded at this extravagant idea of installing a stove in his manor. It would have seemed more natural to him to serve his dogs their food on silver plate. Then, with the full strength of his vigorous lungs, he uttered a huge laugh, saying over and over:

'A stove, here! A stove, here! Ha! Ha! Ha! What a crazy idea!'

She persisted:

'But I tell you it's freezing, my dear; you don't notice, since you're always moving around, but it's freezing.'

He replied, still laughing:

'Pooh! You get used to it, and anyway it's very good for the health. You'll feel all the better for it. We're not Parisians, hang it all! We don't need to live huddled round the fire. Anyway, spring is just round the corner.'

Around the beginning of January, something terrible happened: her father and mother died in a coach accident. She went to Paris for the funeral. And her grief preoccupied her for about six months.

The fine warm sunny days finally roused her a little, and she let herself languish mournfully on until the autumn.

When the cold weather returned, she faced up to the dark future for the first time. What would she do? Nothing. What was there left for her now? Nothing. What expectation, what hope could bring her heart back to life? None. A doctor she consulted had declared that she would never have children.

The cold, more bitter and biting than the previous year, made her suffer continually. She would stretch her shivering hands out to the leaping flames. The blazing fire burnt her face; but icy gusts of air seemed to blow up and down her spine, penetrating the space between her flesh and the fabric of her dress. And she shuddered from head to toe. Countless draughts seemed to have taken up residence in every room – draughts with a life of their own, sly and as tenacious as enemies. She encountered them at every moment; they blew at her ceaselessly, sometimes into her face, sometimes onto her hands, sometimes onto her neck, with their insidious and icy hatred.

She again mentioned getting a stove; but her husband listened to her as if she had been asking for the moon. Installing a piece of equipment like that in Parville seemed to him as impossible as discovering the philosophers' stone.

One day when he had been to Rouen on business, he brought back for his wife a nice little footwarmer that he laughingly called a 'portable stove'; and he deemed this would now be quite enough to stop her from ever feeling the cold again.

Around the end of December, she realised she couldn't go on living like this, and she timidly asked him, one evening:

'Aren't we going to spend a week or two in Paris before the spring comes, my dear?'

He was stupefied.

'Paris? Paris? Whatever for? You must be joking! We're far too comfortable here, in our own home. What strange ideas you sometimes have!'

She stammered:

'It would take our mind off things a bit.'

He just couldn't understand:

'What do you need to take your mind off? Theatres, parties, dinners in town? But you knew perfectly well when you came here that you couldn't expect such amusements!'

She sensed a reproach in these words and the tone in which they were said. She fell silent. She was timid and sweet-tempered, without rebelliousness and without willfulness.

In January, the cold weather came back in all its ferocity. Then snow covered the earth.

One evening, as she was watching the great flock of crows wheeling in formation round the trees, she began, in spite of herself, to cry.

Her husband came in. He asked in surprise:

'What on earth is the matter with you?'

He was happy, perfectly happy; he had never dreamt of any other life or any different pleasures. He had been born in this gloomy countryside, he had grown up here, he liked it and felt at home, comfortable in body and mind.

He couldn't understand how anyone could long for a bit of excitement, or hunger for new and different joys; he couldn't understand that it doesn't seem natural to certain people to stay in the same place for each of the four seasons; he didn't seem to know that spring, summer, autumn and winter bring, for multitudes of people, new pleasures and the experience of new countries.

She couldn't think of anything to say in reply and quickly wiped her eyes. Finally, at her wits' end, she stammered:

'I'm… I… I'm feeling a bit low… I'm a bit bored…'

But she was suddenly terror-stricken at having said that, and she hastily added:

'And then… I'm… I'm a bit cold.'

At these words he grew angry.

'Oh there you go again! You and your stove! Look here, damn it, you haven't had a single cold all the time you've been here!'

Night fell. She went up into her room, for she had insisted on having a separate bedroom. She went to bed. Even in her bed she was cold. She reflected:

'It's always going to be the same, always, until the day I die.'

And she thought of her husband. How could he have said that to her? 'You haven't had a single cold all the time you've been here!'

So she would have to fall ill, start coughing, if he was to understand that she was suffering!

And she was seized with indignation, the exasperation of a weak and timid woman.

She would have to start coughing. Then, no doubt, he would take pity on her. Very well, she would start coughing! He would hear her coughing; he'd have to summon the doctor; he'd see, that husband of hers, he'd see!

She had got out of bed bare-legged and barefoot, and a childish idea made her smile:

'I want a stove, and I'm going to get one. I'll cough so much that he'll have to agree to put one in.'

And she sat down almost naked on a chair. She waited one hour, two hours. She was shivering, but she didn't seem to be catching a cold. Then she decided to use more drastic means.

She soundlessly left her room, went downstairs, opened the door into the garden.

The earth, shrouded in snow, seemed dead. She suddenly stuck out her bare foot and sank it into that light and icy foam. A sensation of cold, as painful as a wound, rose up to her heart; nonetheless, she stretched out her other leg and started to go down the steps, slowly.

Then she walked across the lawn, telling herself:

'I'll go as far as the pine trees.'

She took small steps, breathing heavily, catching her breath each time she sank her bare foot into the snow.

She reached out to touch the first pine tree with her hand, as if to convince herself that she really had carried out her plan in full; then she came back. She thought a couple of times that she was going to fall over, she felt so numb and faint. But before she reached the house, she sat down in that icy foam, and even picked up a handful to rub her chest with.

Then she entered the house and went to bed. It seemed to her, after an hour, as if she had an ant's nest in her throat.

Other ants were running up and down her limbs. Still, she managed to sleep.

The next morning she was coughing, and she was unable to get up.

She fell ill with pneumonia. She started raving, and in her delirium she kept asking for a stove. The doctor demanded that one be installed. Henry gave way, but angrily and reluctantly.

She got no better. Her lungs were severely affected and there were anxieties for her life.

'If she stays here, she won't last out the cold weather,' said the doctor.

They sent her to the south of France.

She went to Cannes, discovered the sunlight, fell in love with the sea, breathed in the perfume of the flowering orange trees.

Then, in the spring, she returned to the north.

But then she was living with the fear of recovering her health, the fear of the long Normandy winters; and as soon as she started to feel better, she would open her window, at night, and dream of the warm shores of the Mediterranean.

Now she is dying. She knows it. She is happy.

She opens out a paper she hadn't looked at, and reads this headline: 'First snow in Paris'.

She shudders, and then she smiles. She gazes at the Esterel over there, turning pink in the sunset; she gazes at the vast blue sky, so blue, the vast blue sea, so blue; and she rises to her feet.

And then she slowly walks back, stopping only to cough, for she has stayed outside for too long, and she has got cold, just a little cold.

She finds a letter from her husband. She opens it, still smiling, and reads:

My dear,
I hope you are well and not missing our lovely part of the world too much. For a few days we've had a heavy frost, so the snow will soon be here. I love this weather and you can bet I certainly don't light your wretched stove...

She stops reading, filled with happiness at the idea that she finally got her stove. Her right hand, the one holding the letter, falls slowly back onto her knees, while she brings her left hand up to her mouth as if to calm the stubborn cough that racks her breast.

Rose

The two young women look as if they have been buried beneath a layer of flowers. They are alone in the huge landau loaded with bouquets as if it were a giant basket. On the front seat, two small hampers of white satin are full of Nice violets, and on the bearskin rug covering the women's knees there is a heap of flowers – roses, mimosas, gillyflowers, daisies, tuberoses and orange blossom, tied together with silk ribbons – which seems to crush their two delicate bodies, so that there emerge from this dazzling, sweet-smelling bed only their shoulders, their arms and a small patch of their blouses, the one blue and the other lilac.

The coachman's whip is sheathed in anemones, the horses' traces are upholstered with wallflowers, the spokes of the wheels are decorated with reseda, and in place of the lamps, two enormous round bouquets seem like the two strange eyes of this flowery beast as it rolls along.

The landau trots smartly along the road, the rue d'Antibes, preceded, followed and accompanied by a host of other carriages bedecked with garlands, filled with women buried under a flood of violets. For it is the flower festival in Cannes.

They reach the boulevard de la Foncière, where the battle takes place. All along the immense avenue a double row of garlanded carriages comes and goes like an endless ribbon. People hurl flowers at each other from carriage to carriage. The flowers fly through the air like bullets, striking the fresh-faced girls, then spinning down and falling into the dust where an army of street urchins picks them up.

A dense crowd watches, noisy but orderly, drawn up on the pavements, and kept in place by the gendarmes on horseback who ride by brutally and push back the over-curious with their feet, as if to prevent the scoundrelly commoners from mixing with the rich.

In the carriages, people call out to each other, recognise one another, and pelt each other with roses. A chariot full of pretty women, dressed in red like devils, draws every eye with their glamorous allure. A gentleman who resembles the portraits of Henri IV energetically and joyfully flings a huge bouquet attached to a piece of elastic. Threatened with the impact, the women hide their eyes and the men lower their heads, but the graceful projectile, rapid and docile, describes a curve and returns to its master who immediately throws it at a new face.

The two young women fling their arsenal out by the handful and receive a hail of bouquets; then, after an hour of battle, finally feeling a little tired, they order the coachman to take the road to the Gulf of St Juan, a road which follows the shore.

The sun disappears behind the Esterel, outlining against its fiery red setting the black, jagged silhouette of the long mountain. The calm sea stretches out, blue and clear, as far as the horizon where it merges into the sky, and the fleet, anchored in the middle of the gulf, looks like a herd of monstrous beasts, motionless on the water, apocalyptic animals, armoured and humpbacked, topped with masts as frail as feathers, with eyes that light up when night comes.

The young women, stretched out under the heavy fur rug, gaze languidly ahead. Finally, the one says:

'There really are delightful evenings when everything seems really splendid. Don't you think so, Marguerite?'

The other replied:

'Yes, it's splendid all right. But there's always something missing.'

'What could be missing? *I* feel completely happy. I don't need anything more.'

'Oh yes you do. You're not thinking. However great the well-being that lulls our bodies, we always desire something more… for our hearts.'

And the other, with a smile:

'A bit of love?'

'Yes.'

They fell silent, gazing ahead, then the one called Marguerite murmured:

'Life doesn't seem tolerable to me without that. I need to be loved, even if only by a dog. And all of us women are the same – whatever you may say, Simone.'

'I don't agree, my dear. I prefer not to be loved at all rather than to be loved by just anybody. Do you think it would be pleasant for me to be loved, for instance, by… by…'

She tried to think of someone who might love her, looking over the vast landscape. Her eyes, after having followed the circle of the horizon, fell onto two metal buttons gleaming on the coachman's back, and she continued, with a laugh: 'by my coachman'.

Mme Margot barely smiled and in a low voice uttered the words:

'I can assure you that it's great fun being loved by a servant. It's happened to me two or three times. They roll their eyes in such a funny way that it's enough to make you die of laughing. Of course, you have to behave all the more strictly to them the more deeply in love they are, then you show them the door, one day, on the first pretext that presents itself, since you'd look ridiculous if anyone noticed.'

Mme Simone was listening, her eyes staring ahead, then she declared:

'No, on second thoughts, the heart of my footman would certainly not be enough for me. So tell me how you realised they were in love with you.'

'I realised the same way as with other men, when they started behaving stupidly.'

'The others don't seem to me so silly when they love me.'

'They are idiots, my dear, unable to make small talk, to reply to your questions, to understand anything at all.'

'But what was it like when you were loved by a servant? You were – well, what? Touched? Flattered?'

'Touched? No. Flattered? Yes, a little. One is always flattered by the love of a man, whoever it is.'

'Come off it, Margot!'

'Oh yes one is. Look, I'll tell you about a strange thing that happened to me. You'll see how weird and confusing are the things that go on inside us in cases like this.

'It will be four years ago this coming autumn, I happened to be without a chambermaid. I tried five or six, one after another, who were perfectly useless, and had almost given up all hope of finding one when I read, in the small ads of a paper, that a young girl, able to sew, embroider and dress hair, was looking for a position, and that she could provide the best references. What's more, she could speak English.

'I wrote to the address indicated, and, the next day, the person in question presented herself. She was quite tall, slender, a little pale, very timid in manner. She had lovely dark eyes, a charming complexion, and I took to her straight away. I asked for her references: she gave me one in English, for she had just left, she said, the house of Lady Rymwell where she had been for ten years.

'The reference attested that the girl had left of her own accord to return to France, and that she had given them no cause for complaint, throughout her long period of service, other than a little "French coquettishness".

'This straitlaced English turn of phrase even made me smile a little and I immediately retained the services of this chambermaid.

'She moved into my house the very same day; her name was Rose.

'A month later, I adored her.

'She was a real find, a pearl, a phenomenon.

'She could dress my hair with the most exquisite taste; she could arrange the lace of a hat better than the best milliners and she was even a good dressmaker.

'I was stupefied by her skills. I had never been so well served.

'She would dress me rapidly, with amazingly agile hands. Never once did I feel her fingers on my skin, and nothing is more unpleasant to me than the contact of a servant-girl's hand. I soon fell into the habit of being extremely lazy, as it was pleasant to let myself be dressed, from head to toe, and from blouse to gloves, by this tall and timid girl, always blushing slightly, and never saying a word. When I got out of my bath, she would rub me down and massage me while I lay in a light doze on my couch; my word, I viewed her more as a somewhat lower-class friend than as a mere domestic.

'Well, one morning, my concierge mysteriously asked to have a private word with me. I was surprised, and had him brought in. He was a very reliable man, an old soldier, my husband's former adjutant.

'He seemed embarrassed at what he had to say. Finally, he stammered out:

'"Madame, an inspector from the local police station is downstairs."

'I asked sharply:

' "What does he want?" '

' "He wants to carry out a search of the house." '

'Of course the police are useful, but I hate them. I don't think it's a very noble occupation. And I replied, as much angry as offended:

' "A search? Why? Whatever for? He's not to come in." '

'The concierge replied:

' "He claims there's a criminal hiding here." '

'This time I was afraid and I ordered him to bring the police inspector to me so he could explain. He was quite a well brought-up man, decorated with the Legion of Honour. He apologised, begged my pardon, then told me that I had a convict on my staff!

'I was quite disgusted; I replied that I could speak for everyone on my staff and I went through them one by one.

' "The concierge, Pierre Courtin, an ex-soldier." '

' "It's not him." '

' "The coachman, François Pingau, a peasant from the Champagne region, the son of one of my father's farmers." '

' "It's not him." '

' "A stable-boy, also from Champagne, and also the son of peasants I know, plus a footman you have just seen." '

' "It's not him." '

' "Well, Monsieur, you can see you must be mistaken." '

' "I'm sorry, Madame, I'm sure I'm *not* mistaken. As it's a dangerous criminal we're after, would you please be so kind as to summon here, into your presence and mine, your whole staff?" '

'I resisted at first, then I gave way, and I ordered all my staff to come up, men and women.

'The police inspector took them all in at a single glance, then declared:

' "That's not everyone."

' "I'm sorry, Monsieur, there's only my chambermaid, a young girl you could never take for a convict."

'He asked:

' "May I see her too?"

' "Certainly."

'I rang for Rose, who immediately appeared. Hardly had she come in than the inspector made a sign, and two men I hadn't seen, hiding behind the door, flung themselves on her, grabbed her hands and tied them up with rope.

'I uttered a cry of fury, and made as if to leap forward to defend her. The inspector stopped me.

' "This girl, Madame, is a man by the name of Jean-Nicolas Lecapet, sentenced to death in 1879 for rape and murder. His sentence was commuted to life imprisonment. He escaped four months ago. We've been after him ever since."

'I was flabbergasted, thunderstruck. I couldn't believe it. The inspector continued, with a laugh:

' "I can give you just one proof. He has a tattoo on his right arm."

'They rolled up his sleeve. It was true. The policeman added with a certain lack of taste:

' "You can trust us to check out his other particulars."

'And they led away my chambermaid!

'Well, would you believe it, my main emotion wasn't anger at having been taken in like that, deceived and made fun of; it wasn't the shame of having been dressed, undressed, handled and touched by that man... but a... deep humiliation... humiliation as a woman. Do you understand?'

'Not really, no.'

'Come on... Think about it... That fellow had been sentenced... for rape... Well, I kept thinking... about the

woman he had raped... and that was... what humiliated me...
There you have it... Now do you understand?'

And Mme Simone did not reply. She gazed straight ahead,
with a fixed and singular expression in her eyes as she stared at
the two gleaming buttons on the coachman's livery, with that
sphinx-like smile that women sometimes have.

The Dowry

No one was surprised when Simon Lebrument married Mlle Jeanne Cordier. Maître Lebrument had just purchased the notary practice of Maître Papillon; naturally he needed money to pay for it, and Mlle Jeanne Cordier had three hundred thousand francs in ready cash, banknotes and bearer bonds.

Maître Lebrument was a handsome young man, who had a certain charm about him, a notary charm, a provincial charm, but a charm all the same – which was rare in Boutigny-le-Rebours.

Mlle Cordier was a graceful, fresh young woman, a bit gauche in her gracefulness and a bit dowdy in her freshness, but she was, all in all, a pretty girl, desirable and well worth fêting.

The wedding ceremony threw Boutigny into a turmoil of activity.

The newly-weds were the object of considerable admiration as they returned to enjoy their happiness in the privacy of their conjugal home, having decided to take just a short trip to Paris after a few days of intimacy together.

This period of intimacy was quite charming, since Maître Lebrument managed to bring to his first close acquaintance with his wife a skill, a delicacy and a tact that were altogether remarkable. He had adopted as his motto: 'All things come to those who wait.' He knew how to be patient and passionate at the same time. His success was rapid and complete.

After four days, Mme Lebrument was head-over-heels in love with her husband. She couldn't do a thing without him, she needed to have him near her all day long so she could hug him, kiss him, paw his hands, his beard, his nose, etc. She would sit on his knees and, taking him by the ears, say: 'Open your mouth and close your eyes.' He would trustingly open his mouth, half close his eyes, and be given a long loving lingering kiss, which sent great shivers up and down his spine. And he in turn didn't have enough caresses, enough lips, enough hands, enough anything; his whole person was not enough to fête his wife from morning to evening and evening to morning.

One day, after the first week had gone by, he said to his young partner:

'If you like, we can leave for Paris next Tuesday. We'll do what lovers do when they're not married: we'll go to restaurants, the theatre, the cabarets – just everywhere!'

She leapt for joy.

'Oh yes! Oh yes! Let's go as soon as possible.'

He continued:

'And then, since we mustn't forget anything, tell your father to keep your dowry ready; I'll take it with us and use the opportunity to pay off Maître Papillon.'

'I'll tell him tomorrow morning,' she said.

And he clasped her in his arms to dally affectionately with her again, just the way she had got to like over the past week.

The following Tuesday, the father- and mother-in-law saw their daughter and son-in-law off at the station, where they were taking the train to the capital.

His father-in-law was saying:

'I swear it is taking such a risk to carry so much money in your briefcase.'

And the young notary smiled.

'Don't worry about a thing, papa, I'm used to things like this. You must understand that, in my profession, it so happens that I sometimes carry almost a million francs. In that way, we at least avoid a whole load of formalities and delays. Don't worry about it.'

The stationmaster was shouting:

'Passengers for Paris, all aboard!'

They hurried into a compartment where there were two old women.

Lebrument murmured in his wife's ear:

'What a bore. I won't be able to smoke.'

She replied in a low tone:

'Yes, *I* think it's a bore too: but not because of your cigar.'

The train gave a whistle and pulled out of the station. The journey lasted an hour, during which they didn't say much, as the two old women stayed wide awake.

As soon as they had arrived in the square in front of the Saint-Lazare station, Maître Lebrument said to his wife:

'If you like, darling, we can go and have lunch on the boulevard: then we'll come back and pick up our suitcase and take it to the hotel in our own time.'

She immediately agreed.

'Oh yes, let's go and have lunch in the restaurant. Is it far?'

He replied:

'A fair way, but we can take the bus.'

She was surprised.

'Why don't we hire a cab?'

He started to scold her with a smile.

'So that's how you save money! A cab for a five-minute journey, at six sous per minute – you'd be really splashing out!'

'That's true,' she said, a little taken aback.

A big omnibus was speeding by, drawn by three trotting horses. Lebrument shouted:

'Driver! Hey, driver!'

The heavy carriage halted. And the young notary, pushing

his wife forward, said to her rapidly:

'Go inside, I'm going up on top so I can at least smoke a cigarette before lunch.'

She had no time to reply; the driver, who'd seized her by the arm to help her climb onto the footboard, quickly pushed her into his vehicle, and she fell, all in a dazed heap, onto a seat, looking on in stupor as her husband's feet, from behind the rear window, climbed up to the top deck.

And there she sat, motionless, between a fat gentleman who smelt of pipe smoke, and an old woman who smelt of dog.

All the other passengers, sitting in silent rows – an apprentice grocer, a working-class woman, an infantry sergeant, a gentleman with gold-rimmed glasses wearing a silk hat with a huge brim curved up like gutter pipes, two self-important and grumpy ladies who seemed to be saying, from the way they sat: 'We are here, but we deserve better', two nuns, a woman with her hair down, and an undertaker – looked like a collection of caricatures, or a gallery of grotesques in a museum, or a series of satirical cartoons of the human face, like those rows of comical targets that people throw balls at in fairgrounds.

The vehicle's jolts set their heads bouncing up and down, making them shake and the flaccid skin on their cheeks quiver; and as the vibration of the wheels began to numb them, they had the air of stupefied, somnolent idiots.

The young woman sat there inert.

'Why didn't he come and sit with me?' she kept asking herself. A vague sadness oppressed her. He really could have gone without that cigarette, after all.

The nuns signalled for the bus to stop, and got out one after the other, emitting the musty odour of old skirts.

The bus set off, then stopped again. And a cook got in, a red-faced woman, panting heavily. She sat down and plumped her shopping basket on her knees. A strong smell of washing-up water spread through the carriage.

'It's further than I'd have imagined,' thought Jeanne.

The undertaker got off and was replaced by a coachman who smelt of stables. The girl with her hair down was replaced by a messenger whose feet gave off the aroma of his errands.

The notary's wife felt ill at ease, nauseous, on the verge of tears without knowing why.

Other people got off, and new ones got on. The bus kept on going, along endless streets, halting at all the stops before starting off again.

'How far it is!' Jeanne kept saying to herself. 'So long as he hasn't been distracted by something, or dozed off! He's been wearing himself out these last few days.'

Little by little all the passengers got off. She remained alone, all alone. The driver shouted:

'Vaugirard!'

As she did not move, he repeated:

'Vaugirard!'

She stared at him, realising that he was talking to her, since there was no one else left on the bus. The man repeated, for the third time:

'Vaugirard!'

Then she asked:

'Where are we?'

He replied grumpily:

'We're at Vaugirard, for heaven's sake! I must've told you twenty times.'

'Is it a long way to the boulevard?' she asked.

'Which boulevard?'

'The boulevard des Italiens!'

'We went past there ages ago!'

'Oh! Could you please tell my husband?'

'Your husband? And where might he be?'

'On the top deck.'

'On the top deck? But everyone got down off there ages ago.'

She started with terror.

'What? That's impossible! He got on with me! Go and have a look; he must be there!'

The driver started to get really rude.

'Come on, little lady, stop blabbering. One's gone, another ten'll soon be along. Hop it, we're at the end of the line. You'll soon pick another one up in the streets.'

Tears rose to her eyes. She persisted:

'But Monsieur, you're wrong, I can assure you that you're wrong. He was carrying a big briefcase under his arm.'

The bus driver started to laugh.

'A big briefcase? Oh yes! He got off at la Madeleine. That's how it is: he's dumped you! Ha! Ha! Ha!…'

The carriage had come to a halt. She got off, and, in spite of herself, instinctively shot a glance up at the roof of the omnibus. It was totally deserted.

Then she burst into tears, and said aloud, without thinking that people were looking and listening to her:

'What will become of me?'

The inspector of the omnibus office came up.

'What's the matter?'

The driver replied roguishly:

'It's a lady that her husband has abandoned en route.'

The other said:

'Fine, don't bother about that, just carry on with your job.'

And he turned on his heels.

Then she started to walk along at random, too appalled, too dismayed even to understand what was happening to her. Where could she go? What could she do? What had happened to her? How had such a mistake, such an attack of forgetfulness, such a misapprehension, such an incredible fit of absent-mindedness come about?

She had two francs in her pocket. Who could she turn to? And all at once, she remembered her cousin Barral, deputy head of a department in the naval ministry.

She had just enough to pay for the cab journey; she had herself driven to his home. And she caught him just as he was leaving for his ministry. He was carrying, as did Lebrument, a big briefcase under his arm.

She leapt out of her carriage.

'Henry!' she cried.

He stopped, stupefied.

'Jeanne?... Here?... All by yourself?... What are you doing? Where have you come from?'

She stammered, her eyes full of tears:

'My husband has just got lost.'

'Lost? Where?'

'On an omnibus.'

'On an omnibus?... Oh!...'

And as she wept she told him all that had happened.

He listened reflectively. He asked:

'This morning, he seemed quite calm and clear-headed?'

'Yes.'

'Right. Did he have a lot of money on him?'

'Yes, he was carrying my dowry.'

'Your dowry?... All of it?'

'Yes, all of it... so he could pay immediately for the notary practice.'

'Well, my dear cousin, right now your husband must be heading as fast as he can in the direction of Belgium.'

She still didn't understand. She stammered:

'My husband... what did you say?...'

'I'm saying he's made off with your... your capital. That's all.'

She stood there, choked, murmuring:

'Then he's... he's... he's a miserable wretch!...'

Then, coming over all weak with the intensity of her feelings, she fell on her cousin's waistcoat, sobbing.

As people were stopping to look at them, he gently pushed her into the entrance of his house and, holding her up by the waist, made her climb the staircase and, as his thunderstruck maid opened the door, he ordered:

'Sophie, run over to the restaurant to fetch lunch for two. I'm not going into the ministry today.'

Bed 29

When Captain Epivent went by in the street, all the women turned round. He really presented the perfect example of a handsome officer of the hussars. So he was always parading and strutting up and down, filled with pride and preoccupied with his thighs, his waist and his moustache. And they were superb, too, moustache, waist and thighs. The first was blond, very prominent, falling martially onto his upper lip in a fine wave the colour of ripe hay, but slender, meticulously curled, and swooping down on either side of his mouth in two powerful bristling sweeps that positively swaggered. His waist was as slender as if he had been wearing a corset, while a powerful masculine torso, broad chest thrown out, rose above it. His thighs were admirable, the thighs of a gymnast, a dancer; every ripple of their muscular flesh showed through the tight-fitting fabric of his red trousers.

He marched along stiff-legged, feet and arms turned out, with that slightly swaying gait of cavalrymen, which is well suited to show off the legs and the torso, and seems so very impressive on a man in a uniform, but commonplace on someone in a frock-coat.

Like many officers, Captain Epivent did not look good in civilian clothes. He made no more of an impression than a shop assistant when he was dressed in grey or black flannels. But in uniform, he triumphed. He had a fine head, too, with a slender, curved nose, blue eyes and a narrow forehead. He was bald, it's true, though he never understood why his hair had fallen out. He took consolation in the thought that with big moustaches, a somewhat bare cranium doesn't look bad at all.

He despised everyone in general, but there were many gradations to his contempt.

To begin with, as far as he was concerned, the middle classes didn't exist. He looked at them the same way one looks at animals, without granting them any more attention than one grants sparrows or hens. Only officers counted in the world, but he didn't feel the same esteem for *all* officers. He respected, in fact, only the handsome ones, since the one true quality of a military man should be his imposing appearance. A soldier was a strapping lad, devil take it, a great strapping lad made to make love and war, a man who could pack a punch, handle a horse and woo a woman – no more, no less. He classified the generals of the French army in accordance with their waistline, their bearing and the rebarbative appearance of their face. Bourbaki seemed to him to be the greatest man of war of modern times.[1]

He laughed uproariously at officers of the line who are short and fat and pant as they march, but above all he had an invincibly low opinion, bordering on repugnance, for the poor puny types who graduated from the Ecole Polytechnique, those skinny little bespectacled men, clumsy and maladroit, who seem about as able to wear a uniform as a rabbit is to say mass – to use his own words. He was indignant that the army should tolerate the presence of these little squits with their matchstick legs, who walk like crabs, don't drink, don't eat much, and seem to prefer equations to pretty women.

Captain Epivent was constantly meeting with success and celebrating triumphs over the fair sex.

Every time he was dining in the company of a woman, he considered himself certain to finish the night engaged in a little heart-to-heart with her, on the same mattress; and if insurmountable obstacles prevented him from being victorious that evening, he was at least sure of 'tomorrow's installment'. His friends didn't like letting him meet their mistresses, and the shopkeepers, who had pretty wives working at the counters of their stores, knew him, feared him, and hated him intensely.

When he went by, the saleswoman would, in spite of herself, exchange glances with him through the shop window; one of those glances more eloquent than words of affection, containing as they do an appeal and a reply, a desire and a declaration. And the husband, warned by a kind of instinct, would spin round on his heels, and stare furiously at the proud, strutting silhouette of the officer. And when the captain had gone by, smiling and pleased with the effect he had created, the shopkeeper, edgily sweeping away the objects spread out in front of him, would declare:

'Look at that great turkeycock. When are they going to stop feeding all those good-for-nothings who parade their tin medals up and down the streets? If you ask me, I prefer a butcher to a soldier. If he has blood on his apron, at least it's the blood of an animal; and a man like that is useful for something; and the knife he carries isn't designed to kill men. I can't understand why they tolerate those public murderers displaying their instruments of death in the streets. I know we have to have them, but at least they should be hidden, and not dressed up like in some masquerade with red trousers and blue jackets. They don't usually dress executioners up, do they?'

The wife, without replying, imperceptibly shrugged her shoulders, while the husband, sensing her gesture without seeing it, exclaimed:

'You need to be off your rocker to go and watch daft nincompoops like that parading up and down!'

Captain Epivent's conquests had at all events given him a well-established reputation throughout the French army.

Now, in 1868, his regiment, the 102nd Hussars, came to Rouen where they were to be stationed.

He was soon a well-known figure in town. He appeared every evening, around five o'clock, on the cours Boïeldieu, to take an absinthe at the Café de la Comédie, but before entering the establishment, he would take care to go for a stroll along the avenue to show off his legs, his waist and his moustache.

The Rouen shopkeepers who were also out for a stroll, their hands behind their backs, preoccupied with business and talking about the ups and downs of the market, would glance at him all the same and murmur:

'Damn it, there's a fine figure of a man.'

Then, when they got to know him:

'Look, it's Captain Epivent! You have to admit, he's a strapping fellow!'

Women, when they crossed his path, made a quite peculiar gesture with their heads, a sort of frisson of modesty as if they felt weak all over or were standing naked in front of him. They lowered their eyes a little with the shadow of a smile on their lips, and with the longing to be found charming and to earn a glance from him. When he was out walking with a man friend, his friend never omitted to murmur with jealous envy, each time he saw the same performance being repeated:

'That blighter Epivent is one hell of a lucky fellow!'

Among the kept women of the town, there was a real struggle, a race, as to who would snap him up. They all came along at five o'clock, the time of the officers' get-together, to the cours Boïeldieu, and they trailed their dresses behind them as they walked two by two up and down the length of the avenue, while, two by two, lieutenants, captains and commanding officers trailed their sabres along the pavement, before going into the café.

Now one evening, 'la belle Irma', mistress, it was said, of M. Templier-Papon, the rich factory owner, had her carriage brought to a halt outside the Comédie, where she got out and seemed to go in to buy some paper, or order some visiting-cards from M. Paulard, the engraver, all so that she could pass in front of the officers' tables and direct at Captain Epivent a glance which meant: 'Whenever you like,' so clearly that Colonel Prune, who was drinking the green liqueur[2] with his lieutenant-colonel, couldn't stop himself grumbling:

'That swine! He's a lucky bastard and no mistake!'

The colonel's exclamation did the rounds; and Captain Epivent, touched by this expression of approval from on high, passed by next day, in full uniform, several times over, beneath the windows of the lovely lady.

She saw him, came to the window, and smiled.

That same evening he was her lover.

They flaunted their relationship, made a spectacle of themselves, compromised each other, both equally proud to be involved in such an adventure.

The affair between la belle Irma and the officer was the sole talk of the town. M. Templier-Papon was the only one to be left in the dark.

Captain Epivent was radiant with triumph; and every moment he would repeat:

'Irma has just told me... Irma said to me last night... yesterday, when I was having dinner with Irma...'

For more than a year, he displayed, exhibited, showed off this love throughout Rouen, like a flag captured from the enemy. He felt he had grown in stature thanks to this conquest; a man who was envied, more sure of the future, more sure of the cross of the Legion of Honour that he so greatly desired, for he was constantly in the public eye, and a high profile is enough to make sure you are not forgotten.

But then war broke out and the captain's regiment was one of the first to be sent to the frontier. The farewell scenes were heartbreaking. They lasted a whole night.

Sabre, red trousers, kepi, and dolman had all been tipped off the back of a chair and scattered on the ground; dresses, skirts, silk stockings were strewn about too, having fallen in disorder, all jumbled up with the uniform on the carpet; the room was topsy-turvy as if a battle had taken place; Irma, quite hysterical, her hair dishevelled, kept throwing her arms in desperation round the officer's neck, holding him tight; then, letting go of him, she would roll around on the ground, knock the furniture over, tear the fringes off the armchairs, and bite their legs, while the captain, deeply affected, but not very skilful at consoling people, kept saying:

'Irma, my little Irma, there's nothing to be said, I just have to go.'

And from time to time he would wipe away with the tip of his finger a tear that had sprung to the corner of his eye.

They separated at dawn. She followed her lover in a carriage until he reached the first stage. And she embraced him almost in full view of the regiment at the moment of separation. The others even thought this was very kind, very right and proper; and his friends shook the captain's hand, exclaiming:

'You lucky blighter, you can't deny the lass had a heart of gold.'

They really saw something patriotic in her gesture.

The regiment was sorely tried during the campaign. The captain conducted himself heroically and finally won his cross; then once the war was over, he returned to garrison life in Rouen.

The minute he was back, he asked for news of Irma, but nobody could give him any precise information.

According to some, she had lived it up with the Prussian staff officers.

According to others, she had retired to the home of her parents, small farmers who lived near Yvetot.

He even sent his adjutant to the town hall to consult the register of deaths. The name of his mistress was not among them.

And he was overwhelmed by a grief which he paraded to all and sundry. He even attributed his sorrow to the enemy, blaming the Prussians who had occupied Rouen for the young woman's disappearance, and declaring:

'When the next war comes along, those scoundrels will pay for this.'

Now one morning, as he was entering the mess at lunch-time, a messenger, an old man in overalls, wearing a waxed cap, delivered an envelope to him. He opened it and read:

Darling,
I'm in hospital, very ill, very ill. Won't you come and see me?
I'd so much like that!

Irma

The Captain turned pale, and moved with pity, he declared:

'God Almighty! The poor girl! I'll go straight after lunch.'

And during the whole meal, he told those at the officers' table that Irma was in hospital; but he was going to get her out, damn and blast it! It was the fault of those Prussian buggers. She must have found herself all alone, penniless, poverty-stricken, as they would certainly have pillaged her furniture.

'Ah, those bastards!'

All were greatly touched by his account.

Hardly had he slipped his table napkin back into its round wooden holder than he rose; and having picked up his sabre from the coat peg, puffing out his chest to give himself a slimmer waist, he fastened his sword-belt, then set off at the double in the direction of the civilian hospital.

But at the door of the hospital building where he had expected he would be given immediate entrance, he was sternly turned away, and even had to go and see his colonel, to whom he explained his situation, and who gave him a note for the hospital manager.

The manager, having forced the handsome captain to hang around in his waiting room for a while, finally gave him a letter of authorisation, with a cold and disapproving bow.

As soon as he reached the door, he felt ill at ease in this asylum of poverty, suffering and death. A porter showed him the way.

He went along on tiptoe, so as not to make any noise, through long corridors where there hung a musty odour of dampness, sickness and medicine. An occasional murmur of voices was the only thing to break the deep silence that reigned throughout the hospital.

Sometimes, through an open door, the Captain would notice a ward, a line of beds with their sheets covering the shape of the bodies in them. Convalescent women, sitting on chairs at the foot of their beds, were sewing, garbed in a uniform of grey canvas and with white bonnets on their heads.

His guide came to a sudden stop in front of one of these galleries filled with patients. On the door could be read, in big letters, 'Syphilitics'. The captain shuddered, then he felt himself blush. A nurse was preparing some medicine on a small wooden table at the entrance.

'I'll take you there,' she said. 'It's bed 29.'

And she started to lead the way, as the officer followed.

Then she pointed to a narrow bed.

'It's there.'

Nothing was visible but a swelling of the blankets. Even the head was concealed under the sheet.

On all sides, faces rose above the beds – pale faces, filled with astonishment as they gazed at the uniform; the faces of women, young women and old women, but all of them looking ugly and vulgar, in their loose regulation working jackets.

The captain, deeply disturbed, holding his sabre in one hand and his kepi in the other, murmured:

'Irma.'

There was a commotion in the bed and his mistress' face appeared, but so changed, so tired, so thin, that he didn't recognise her.

She was breathing heavily, choked by emotion, and managed to utter the words:

'Albert!... Albert!... It's you!... Oh!... How nice... how nice...'

And tears flowed from her eyes.

The nurse brought up a chair.

'Take a seat, Monsieur.'

He sat down, and looked at the face, pale and so wretched, of this woman he had left looking so beautiful and fresh.

He said:

'What's been the matter with you?'

She replied, as she continued to weep:

'You saw it perfectly well, it's written on the door.'

And she hid her eyes with the edge of her sheets.

He continued, flabbergasted and filled with shame:

'However did you catch that, my poor girl?'

She murmured:

'It was those Prussian bastards. They practically took me by force and infected me.'

He could think of nothing else to say. He gazed at her and kept turning his kepi round and round on his knees.

The other patients continued to stare at him, and he thought he could detect an odour of rottenness, the odour of corrupt flesh and infamy in this ward full of women afflicted by the foul and terrible disease.

She murmured:

'I don't think I'm going to pull through. The doctor says it's really serious.'

Then, spotting the cross on the officer's chest, she exclaimed:

'Oh! You've won a medal! I'm so pleased! I'm so pleased! Can I give you a kiss?'

A shudder of fear and disgust ran over the Captain's skin at the thought of this kiss.

He wanted to get away right now, to be out in the open air, not to have to see any more of this woman. But he lingered on, not knowing how to get up and say his farewells. He stammered:

'So you didn't get treatment.'

A flame flickered in Irma's eyes. 'No, I wanted to take my revenge, even if it meant I had to snuff it myself! And I infected them in turn, each and every one of them, as many as I could. As long as they were in Rouen I didn't get treatment.'

He declared, in embarrassed tones, though with a hint of gaiety:

'Well you did the right thing there.'

She said, growing more animated, her face glowing red at the cheek-bones:

'Oh yes: more than one of them will die thanks to me, you can count on it. I can assure you I took my revenge.'

He uttered the words:

'So much the better.'

Then, rising to his feet:

'Well, I'm going to have to leave you, I have to be at the colonel's at four o'clock.'

She reacted with surprise and disappointment.

'Already! You're leaving me already! But you've only just got here!…'

But he wanted to get away at any price.

'You can see that I came straight away; but I absolutely must be at the colonel's at four o'clock.'

She asked:

'Is it still Colonel Prune?'

'It's still him. He was wounded twice.'

She continued:

'And what about your friends, were there any killed?'

'Yes. Saint-Timon, Savagnat, Poli, Sapreval, Robert, de Courson, Pasafil, Santal, Caravan and Poivron are dead. Sahel had his arm blown off and Courvoisin had a leg crushed; Paquet lost his right eye.'

She listened, deeply interested. Then, suddenly, she stammered:

'Will you give me a kiss, please, before you leave me? Mme Langlois isn't here.'

And in spite of the disgust that rose to his lips, he placed them on that pallid forehead, while she, flinging her arms around him, planted passionate kisses on the blue fabric of his dolman.

She resumed:

'You'll come back, won't you, you'll come back? Promise me you'll come back!'

'Yes, I promise.'

'When? Can you make Thursday?'

'Yes, Thursday.'

'Thursday at two.'

'Yes, Thursday at two.'

'You promise me?'

'I promise you.'

'Goodbye, darling.'

'Goodbye.'

And he left, disconcerted, under the gaze of the whole ward, holding his head low to try and look smaller; and when he was out in the street, he took a deep breath.

That evening, his comrades asked him:

'Well? What about Irma?'

He replied, with some embarrassment:

'She's had pneumonia, she's very ill.'

But a little lieutenant, sniffing something from the captain's demeanour, went to make enquiries, and the next day, when the captain walked into the mess, he was greeted by a salvo of laughs and jokes. They were taking their revenge, at last.

They learnt, in addition, that Irma had lived it up quite frantically with the Prussian staff officers, that she'd gone galloping round the whole area with a colonel in the Blue Hussars and plenty of others besides, and that in Rouen, they'd called her nothing but 'the Prussians' woman'.

For a whole week, the captain was victimised by the regiment. He kept receiving, through the post, revelatory notes, prescriptions, the names and addresses of specialist doctors, even parcels of medicine the nature of which was clearly written on the label.

And the colonel, once he had been informed, declared in stern tones:

'Well, well, the captain had a fine acquaintance there. I'll have to compliment him on his choice.'

After nearly two weeks, the captain received another letter from Irma asking him to come. He tore it up with rage and did not reply.

A week later, she wrote to him again saying that she was really very ill, and wanted to say goodbye to him.

He did not reply.

Another few days elapsed, and he received a visit from the chaplain of the hospital.

The woman called Irma Pavolin, on her deathbed, was begging him to come.

He did not dare refuse to follow the chaplain, but he entered the hospital with a heart swollen with vicious rancour, wounded vanity, and humiliated pride.

He found her hardly changed and thought she must have been having him on.

'What do you want from me?' he said.

'I wanted to say goodbye. It seems I'm in a really bad way.'

He didn't believe her.

'Listen, you're making me the laughing-stock of the regiment, and I don't want it to carry on.'

She asked:

'What have *I* done against you?'

He was irritated that he couldn't think of any reply.

'Don't expect me to come back here to have everyone make fun of me!'

She looked at him with her dull eyes in which a pale flame of anger flickered, and she repeated:

'What have *I* done against you? Didn't I treat you kindly, is that it? Did I ever ask you for anything? If it weren't for you, I'd still be with M. Templier-Papon and I wouldn't be here today. Just look here; if anyone has anything to reproach me with, it isn't you.'

He continued, his voice tremulous but forceful:

'I'm not reproaching you for anything, but I can't carry on seeing you. Your behaviour with the Prussians was the shame of the entire town.'

She fell back suddenly in her bed.

'My behaviour with the Prussians? But I've already told you they took me by force, and that, if I didn't get treatment, it was because I wanted to infect them. If I'd wanted to get better, it wouldn't have been difficult, heaven knows! But I wanted to kill them, and I *did* kill quite a few of them, so there!'

He continued to stand there.

'Whichever way, it's still shameful,' he said.

She had a sort of choking fit, then continued:

'What's shameful? Letting myself die so I could exterminate them? Is that it? That's not the way you used to talk when you came to my place in the rue Jeanne d'Arc. Oh! Shameful! *You'd* never have done so much, you and your medal of honour! I deserved it more than you – more than you, I tell you, and I killed more of those Prussians than you did!'

He stood there stupefied in front of her, trembling with indignation.

'Oh shut up!… You know… Shut up… Because… Those things… I won't allow anyone… to cast aspersions…'

But she was hardly listening to him any more.

'You and your medal certainly inflicted such *terrible* damage on the Prussians! Would any of this have happened if you'd managed to stop them getting into Rouen? Well? You were the ones who were supposed to stop them, d'you hear me?[3] And I inflicted more damage on them than you, oh yes I did, much more, since I'm going to die, while *you* go poncing around all tarted up to attract the women...'

On every bed a face was raised and every eye was staring at this man in uniform who was stuttering:

'Shut up... shut up... shut up...'

But she wouldn't shut up. She was shouting:

'Oh you're all swagger, you are, with nothing underneath. I know you, oh yes I do. I know you. Let me tell you I inflicted more damage on them than you did, and I killed more than your whole regiment put together!... Get lost, you... little chicken!'

And scurry away he did, as fast as he could, with great long strides, between the two rows of beds where the syphilitic women were agog. And he could hear the panting, wheezing voice of Irma following him.

'More than you, oh yes, I killed more than you, more than you...'

He came tumbling downstairs four steps at a time, and ran home to hide.

The next day, he learnt she had died.

NOTES

BUTTERBALL

1. A sequence of puns: Loiseau's name is like the French for 'the bird' ('l'oiseau'); 'l'oiseau vole' means both 'the bird flies' and 'the bird thieves', and is also the name of a card-game.

2. 4th September 1870 was the date of the fall of the Second Empire and the declaration of the Third Republic.

3. 'Badinguet' was the nickname of the fallen Emperor, Napoleon III. He was the nephew of Napoleon Bonaparte and his supporters were Bonapartists.

4. Maupassant's arithmetic is incorrect.

5. The number would have been 100 to indicate the W.C.; until the end of the nineteenth century the word *cent* (hundred) was a popular pun on *sent* (it smells, i.e. a toilet).

6. Bertrand du Guesclin (c.1323–80), Breton soldier and constable of France, was an outstanding leader on the French side in the first period of the Hundred Years' War.

7. The son of Napoleon III and the Empress Eugénie was fourteen in 1870.

8. The Marseillaise, associated with the Revolution, was still a subversive song in 1870: it became the French national anthem in 1879, a year before Maupassant wrote this story.

BED 29

1. Charles Bourbaki may have looked the part, but he was an inept general in charge of the French Army of the East in the Franco-Prussian War.

2. The green liqueur is absinthe.

3. Rouen had surrendered without a fight, as we have seen in 'Butterball'.

Guy de Maupassant was born into a noble family in Dieppe in 1850. His parents were separated when he was ten years old and he remained with his mother, Laure le Poittevin, who was to be the inspiration for many of the female characters in his fiction, and who introduced him to her long-time friend Gustave Flaubert, whose scrupulous literary style and psychological realism were profoundly influential on Maupassant's own writing.

In 1869, Maupassant moved to Paris, to a lodging he shared with his father, and enrolled in the university as a law student. With the outbreak of the Franco-Prussian War the following year, however, Maupassant left university and volunteered. He was posted to Rouen and saw service in the freezing Eure countryside; his loathing for the forces of occupation and experiences of petty heroisms and cowardices of this period went on to form the basis for a number of his short stories.

When the war ended in 1872, Flaubert found Maupassant a succession of civil-service jobs and encouraged him to train as a writer. Flaubert's instructions were to write non-stop and not to publish anything. Maupassant stuck to this rule for almost a decade, during which he wrote as instructed and built up a storehouse of experience and observation to be put to use in his later literary output. Flaubert also introduced him to an illustrious literary circle including Emile Zola, Ivan Turgenev and Henry James; with Zola in particular, Maupassant was to form a close friendship and a valuable collaboration.

Finally in 1880 Maupassant's first work was published; it was '*Boule de Suif*' ['Butterball'], included in *Les Soirées de Médan*, a collection of writings on the theme of the war by writers such as Joris-Karl Huysmans, Paul Alexis and Zola.

Maupassant's success was immediate, and journals and papers began to clamour for his work. During the 1880s he wrote some three hundred short stories, a number of novels and travel writings, and a volume of verse. His work was marked by an acute observation of hidden motivations and weaknesses among the bourgeoisie and the lower orders, and often displayed an overt sense of the ridiculous. Among his best-known pieces are the novels *Une vie* ['A Life'], the story of a repressed Norman housewife, and *Bel-Ami*, depicting an unscrupulous and womanising journalist – an allusion to Maupassant himself, who spent some time as a journalist on the newspaper *Le Gaulois*.

Maupassant had suffered from bouts of ill health for many years, and in 1892, the incipient insanity of syphilis led to a suicide attempt. Maupassant was committed to an asylum in Paris, where he spent his last months, alternating between depression and exaltation and claiming psychic powers. He finally died in 1893.

Andrew Brown studied at the University of Cambridge, where he taught French for many years. He now works as a freelance teacher and translator. He is the author of *Roland Barthes: the Figures of Writing* (OUP, 1993) and his translations include *For a Night of Love* by Emile Zola, *The Jinx* by Théophile Gautier, *Mademoiselle de Scudéri* by E.T.A Hoffmann, *Theseus* by André Gide, *Incest* by Marquis de Sade, and *The Ghost-seer* by Friedrich von Schiller, all published by Hesperus Press.

HESPERUS PRESS – 100 PAGES

Hesperus Press, as suggested by the Latin motto, is committed to bringing near what is far – far both in space and time. Works written by the greatest authors, and unjustly neglected or simply little known in the English-speaking world, are made accessible through new translations and a completely fresh editorial approach. Through these short classic works, each around 100 pages in length, the reader will be introduced to the greatest writers from all times and all cultures.

For more information on Hesperus Press, please visit our website: **www.hesperuspress.com**

ET REMOTISSIMA PROPE

SELECTED TITLES FROM HESPERUS PRESS

Gustave Flaubert *Memoirs of a Madman*

Alexander Pope *Scriblerus*

Ugo Foscolo *Last Letters of Jacopo Ortis*

Anton Chekhov *The Story of a Nobody*

Joseph von Eichendorff *Life of a Good-for-nothing*

MarkTwain *The Diary of Adam and Eve*

Giovanni Boccaccio *Life of Dante*

Victor Hugo *The Last Day of a Condemned Man*

Joseph Conrad *Heart of Darkness*

Edgar Allan Poe *Eureka*

Emile Zola *For a Night of Love*

Daniel Defoe *The King of Pirates*

Giacomo Leopardi *Thoughts*

Nikolai Gogol *The Squabble*

Franz Kafka *Metamorphosis*

Herman Melville *The Enchanted Isles*

Leonardo da Vinci *Prophecies*

Charles Baudelaire *On Wine and Hashish*

William MakepeaceThackeray *Rebecca and Rowena*

Wilkie Collins *Who Killed Zebedee?*

Théophile Gautier *The Jinx*

Charles Dickens *The Haunted House*

Luigi Pirandello *Loveless Love*

Fyodor Dostoevsky *Poor People*

E.T.A. Hoffmann *Mademoiselle de Scudéri*

Henry James *In the Cage*

Francis Petrarch *My Secret Book*

André Gide *Theseus*

D.H. Lawrence *The Fox*

Percy Bysshe Shelley *Zastrozzi*

Marquis de Sade *Incest*

Oscar Wilde *The Portrait of Mr W.H.*

Giacomo Casanova *The Duel*

LeoTolstoy *Hadji Murat*

Friedrich von Schiller *The Ghost-seer*

Nathaniel Hawthorne *Rappaccini's Daughter*

Pietro Aretino *The School of Whoredom*

Honoré de Balzac *Colonel Chabert*

Thomas Hardy *Fellow-Townsmen*

Arthur Conan Doyle *The Tragedy of the Korosko*

Stendhal *Memoirs of an Egotist*

Katherine Mansfield *In a German Pension*

Giovanni Verga *Life in the Country*

IvanTurgenev *Faust*

Theodor Storm *The Lake of the Bees*

F. Scott Fitzgerald *The Rich Boy*

Dante Alighieri *New Life*

Charlotte Brontë *The Green Dwarf*

Elizabeth Gaskell *Lois the Witch*

Joris-Karl Huysmans *With the Flow*

George Eliot *Amos Barton*

Gabriele D'Annunzio *The Book of the Virgins*

Heinrich von Kleist *The Marquise of O–*

Alexander Pushkin *Dubrovsky*